Zombies "They're dead. They're all messed up."

BY JOHN SKERCHOCK

Let's talk about zombies! They are the flavor of the month as far as monsters go. After all, there are over a hundred books, thousands of short stories, dozens of comic books, action figures, posters, video and role playing games, movies, and a TV show about them. They are more popular than ever! Yet, it wasn't always so for this monster. If you were to take a poll of monster lovers as to whom their favorite monster is, the Creature from the Black Lagoon would win. Just go to any classic monster website and you'll find out. Yet when it comes to which is the scariest monster out there, the zombie wins hands down. Zombies are the infantry of the monster army. There are thousands of them and, while they are the easiest of monsters to kill, they are also the easiest of monsters to make. They would lead the ranks in an apocalyptic monster invasion. The zombie as we see him today evolved over decades of story telling and low budget horror movies. His origins can be traced to a little low budget film called NIGHT OF THE LIVING DEAD made back in 1968. Directed by George Romero, this movie launched the zombie phenomenon that we see today. In this column we're going to take a look back at the origins of how all of this came to be and see how this creature evolved over the years. In 1967, a group of ambitious people got together to make an independent film. Their goal was to make money and make more films. The easiest film to make was and still is a horror film. At that time it could have been distributed to movie houses and outdoor drive-ins across the country without much difficulty. The original title of the movie was NIGHT OF THE FLESH EATERS and at no time in this movie was the word "zombie" ever used. The producers saw their creatures as ghouls but the movie was not called NIGHT OF THE GHOULS for fear it would be confused with an Ed Wood movie of the same name. The film's monsters or "dead things" were influenced by other sources. One of the most obvious is the movie INVISIBLE INVADERS where invisible aliens possessed the bodies of the recently dead to create havoc and mayhem in an attempt to destroy the world. Richard Matheson's book I AM LEGEND, about a human survivor fighting off nocturnal undead played a part as well, but more importantly though was the Vincent Price movie of the book called THE LAST MAN ON EARTH. Another influence was an Outer Limits TV episode where a couple is stranded in an old farmhouse surrounded by alien possessed tumbleweeds. The aliens kill and then reanimate the farmer in an attempt to communicate with the surviving humans, but they fail. The idea of calling the ghouls "zombies" did not exist in 1968. Before NIGHT OF THE LIVING DEAD, zombies were the victims of voodoo witch doctors. They were corpses reanimated for the purpose of being slave workers. Some classic zombie movies are THE ZOMBIES OF MORA TAU, WHITE ZOMBIE, and ZOMBIES ON BROADWAY. Had it not been for a twist of fate, NIGHT OF THE LIVING DEAD may have faded from public awareness and the world of the Romero zombie may not have happened. It all had to do with the copyright. The producers of the film copyrighted the title and not the film itself. When the first distributor picked it up, he changed the name of the film to NIGHT OF THE LIVING DEAD. The movie went with its new name from distributor to distributor and when the film company failed to receive any royalties, they started a lawsuit only to learn they had screwed up. By allowing the name change, they screwed themselves out of any royalties. The movie was declared public domain. When a television station picks up a package of movies to air, the station owners must pay royalties for the right to air those movies. When a movie is in public domain, no fees need to be paid. Television stations all across America stockpiled public domain movies and showed them often. This way they would make money by selling commercial space while not having to pay any royalties. It wasn't unusual during the late 1960s and early 1970s to see NIGHT OF THE LIVING DEAD several times a week just from one television station alone. The movie began to get a following simply from constant repetition (just like A CHRISTMAS STORY—it bombed at the box office but is an institution today simply because TBS plays it constantly for 24 hours every Christmas). By the time the next event happened, there were already millions of fans prepared for it. In 1973 two movies were released that had an impact on the growing zombie culture: CHILDREN SHOULDN'T PLAY WITH DEAD THINGS and THE CRAZIES (by George Romero). While THE CRAZIES is not a zombie movie, it dealt with people infected by a deadly virus that turned most of them into insane killers (like 28 DAYS LATER with a smaller budget). CHILDREN SHOULDN'T PLAY WITH DEAD THINGS was about a small group of young people who used magic to raise the dead. While their intent was on raising one corpse, they actually raised an entire cemetery full, and these dead were hungry. The 1970s as a whole saw a new form of horror movie evolve: the gore film. Like the two films mentioned above and the low budget TEXAS CHAINSAW MASSACRE, horror movies were becoming graphically violent. New monsters were generating new fears in the country's youth as Leatherface, Michael Myers, and Jason Voorhees were created to claim their first victims. And that's when Romero decided it was time to make another living dead movie.

Romero was becoming known for his graphic violence first in NIGHT OF THE LIVING DEAD and then in THE CRAZIES. With special effects genius Tom Savini (who proved his worth in Romero's MARTIN) Romero could take his undead into new territory. And it was about this time that the dead were being called zombies. Seriously, the violence in NIGHT OF THE LIVING DEAD wasn't all that graphic because a lot of it was unseen. Carl Hardman, one of the producers, told me a lot about the making of this movie at a Monster Bash convention he attended shortly before his death. "Our creatures were eating deli meats in those cannibal scenes but the suggestion was there that they were eating human remains." Carl went on to explain that a mythology was born about the movie that no one bothered refuting. The producers and investors were out $114,000, so they didn't care what anyone thought about the movie. George Romero, however, took advantage of what was being said and ran with it. Hardman said, "We weren't trying to make a statement or break new ground by having a black man as the hero. The fact was that Duane Jones was the best actor for the part. It could easily have been someone else." One scene, often cut for television, showed the naked back and buttocks of a female zombie. This scene was called groundbreaking but was actually put in as a little cheesecake for the drive-in audience. Another big deal made was that the part of the little girl played by Kyra Schon was actually written for a boy. "So what," Carl told me. "Normally when writing a script you do that but then you go with who is available. In this case it was Kyra, the only child available." Coincidentally, Kyra was the daughter of Carl Hardman and Marilyn Eastman. George Romero told the fans what they wanted to hear and many believed that the zombie movies were being made to make a statement. That may have been true about the later ones but not NIGHT OF THE LIVING DEAD. This film did help to set the tone for hundreds of horror movies to come. It's what I refer to as the Gilligan's Island Dilemma: seven people are stranded in a situation beyond their control and they must work together to survive or they all die except for one. After watching a few of these movies, the outcome becomes all too predictable and no matter how good a zombie movie is with production values, it still suffers in the end from lazy story telling. DAWN OF THE DEAD was filmed, mostly, in a mall. Clayton Hill, who was the white shirted zombie who got a good meal near the end of the film and also served as the weapons keeper on the set, told me that the cast and crew assembled in the evening and as soon as the mall closed for the night, they went into action and worked until just before the mall opened. There was a lot of freedom and they didn't have to worry about weather or heating bills because the mall took care of that. Simply put George liked the idea of filming in a mall. At the time he wasn't trying to make a social statement. The fans, however, thought he did so George went with it. DAY OF THE DEAD was Romero's final part of the zombie trilogy. Fans loved it but were horrified at the thought of there being no more zombie movies. Their fears were calmed as other zombie movies came along like RETURN OF THE LIVING DEAD—which put its own spin on the NIGHT OF THE LIVING DEAD mythos—the C.H.U.D. movies, and a whole bunch from Europe. Special effects wizard and actor Tom Savini directed a remake of the original NIGHT OF THE LIVIND DEAD in 1990 (this was to be the first of many remakes). I interviewed Tom in 2002 and he said, "I wanted to direct the remake and George said , 'Okay.' I had issues with the original and questions that I wanted to clear up. The main one being whatever happened to Barbara because you never see her again after she is carried out the door. I didn't get to make all the changes I wanted but I got a few done." Plus Savini, like many of us Baby Boomers, believed that the outcome of the movie would be more positive. In 1968, although the country was dealing with the youth rebellion, millions of Americans still trusted and respected their government. They would have listened to what they were told and they would have banded together to help one another. This feeling was present in a minor way in the original movie, but Savini's intent was to make it stronger. The zombies would not have been left to take over the world some ten years later as they did in DAWN OF THE DEAD. Unfortunately for Savini, most people didn't share his vision and the remake wasn't very successful. By the late 1990s and into the new century, it became the Hollywood norm to call every deranged killer a zombie. The film 28 DAYS LATER was about people infected with a virus that turned them into uncontrollable, murderous lunatics. It didn't kill them and cause them to be resurrected, it simply changed their personalities but that was enough for the Hollywood machine to call them zombies. DAWN OF THE DEAD could have easily been called 28 DAYS AMERICA. In this remake the public was introduced to the fast moving zombie. With little difference from the creatures in 28 DAYS LATER, this new version of the zombie was stronger, fast moving, and insane. In all fairness to zombies, the originals in NIGHT OF THE LIVING DEAD weren't all slow-walking, mindless ones fans saw in the last two parts of Romero's trilogy. Some zombies ran and some were smart enough to use rocks as tools, but eventually a zombie code was created. Fans are divided over the fast moving zombies and the slow moving ones. I favor the slow moving ones because I feel they are more terrifying. Simon Pegg, creator and star of SHAUN OF THE DEAD (my all time favorite zombie movie) hit it on the head when he told the Manchester Guardian in November of 2008: "Zombies don't run! I know it's absurd to debate rules of a reality that does not exist, but this genuinely irks me. It's a misconception that diminishes a classic movie monster. The speedy zombie seems implausible to me, even within the fantastic realm he inhabits. Death is a disability, not a superpower. It's hard to run with a cold, let alone the most debilitating malady of them all. More significantly, the fast zombie is bereft of poetic subtlety. As monsters from the id, zombies win out over vampires and werewolves when it comes to the title of Most Potent Metaphorical Monster. Zombies are our destiny writ large. Slow and steady in their approach, weak, clumsy, often absurd, the zombie relentlessly closes in, unstoppable, intractable."

A NOTE FROM THE GRAVE

Welcome to the second—and probably last—issue of Living Dead Press Presents Magazine. Unfortunately, at the time of this printing, there are no plans to make any more. Why? 'Cause it simply takes too long to put together, and though it was fun, books are what we mostly focus on here at Living Dead Press.

But this issue and the first one are a statement that anything can be done if like-minded people put their minds together. And to make sure this little experiment goes out with a blast, this issue is chock full of horror goodness.

In the following pages, we have interviews with zombie authors Adam Fuchs and Nick Cato, on what they've done and what they hope to do in the future; the sexy Scream Queen Sarah French gives us an in-depth interview on her acting and modeling career, and there are enough book and movie reviews to choke a zombie. We also have a nice pile of horror fiction for you to munch on, some shorter than others, but all will entertain.

Eric S. Brown wrote a Bigfoot story special for this issue, and yours truly tossed in a little gem about the state of the U.S. Is my story true horror? Well, not really, but the next time you have to write a check to pay your house taxes, tell me you don't cringe in fear just a little. Sometimes true life is the most terrifying thing of all!

We also have some fantastic artists interviews and graffiti artist Dark Riddle was nice enough to give us the inside scoop on the infamous "Gothicane."

So from myself and all of the staff who worked on this and the first issue, we hope you enjoy reading them as much as we did making them. One thing we tried to do is make these mags timeless, so that even in a year or more—even five years—from now a new fan can read issue one or two and the information within will be just as relevant as the day it was printed.

From one horror fan to another, stay scared, and good readin'!

Editor

Anthony Giangregorio

EDITOR: ANTHONY GIANGREGORIO

FORMATTER: JESUS "DARK RIDDLE" MORALES

CONTRIBUTING WRITERS:

DANE T. HATCHELL

BRANDON CRACRAFT

JOHN SKERCHOCK

DAVID BERNSTEIN

REBECCA BESSER

NEILA THOMPSON

KELLY M. HUDSON

RICK MOORE

ERIC S. BROWN

TONY SCHAAB

SPECIAL THANKS TO:
ADAM FUCHS
SARAH FRENCH
NICK CATO
SHAWN CONN
JUSTIN COONS

Table of Contents

Copyright © 2011 Living Dead Press
Special thanks to Tom Agnetti for the Cover Art

ISBN Softcover ISBN 13: 978-1-61199-017-1   ISBN 10: 1-61199-017-3

For more information on obtaining additional copies of this book, contact:
www.livingdeadpress.com

YOU GOT TO SHOOT THEM IN THE HEAD!

He goes on to say that speed simplifies the zombie. It's like the difference between someone shouting "Boo!" and hearing the sounds of the floorboards creaking in an upstairs room. Is it the MTV generation that is used to instant gratification and believing that "quicker is better" that's ruining zombie movies? Perhaps it is, because a direct to video sequel to the newer DAY OF THE DEAD remake showed zombies jumping walls and crawling across ceilings. When Romero set about making LAND OF THE DEAD, fans were excited. We got to see Pittsburgh some forty years after the zombie infection. George was trying to make a social statement, this time on purpose, about the Iraqi war even to the point of the human survivors fleeing to Canada. The movie made a lot of money, but fans on the whole, were disappointed. The movie was too preachy and lacked a quality story. In part because he received the money to do it and in part listening to his fan's concerns, George went back to his roots by modernizing NIGHT OF THE LVIING DEAD and creating DIARY OF THE DEAD. In DIARY we learn that the zombie infection has just started so it has no context connection to Romero's first four zombie movies. DIARY was followed by SURVIVAL OF THE DEAD a zombie film that fans either loved or hated. It had no theatrical release in the United States and for months was only available in the US by bootleg or purchase over seas. Is this the end of the zombie movie? Of course not. As you read this article, yet another remake of NIGHT OF THE LIVING DEAD is being made with a release date of summer 2011. This remake takes place in New York and features CGI zombies and survivors holed up in a city apartment. And others want to remake DAY OF THE DEAD using the fast moving zombies. And the TV series THE WALKING DEAD will see its second season later this year, so there will be zombies for years to come. This is not the end of zombies. And someday, if you wish hard enough, you'll become a zombie too!

They're Dead   They're all messed up!

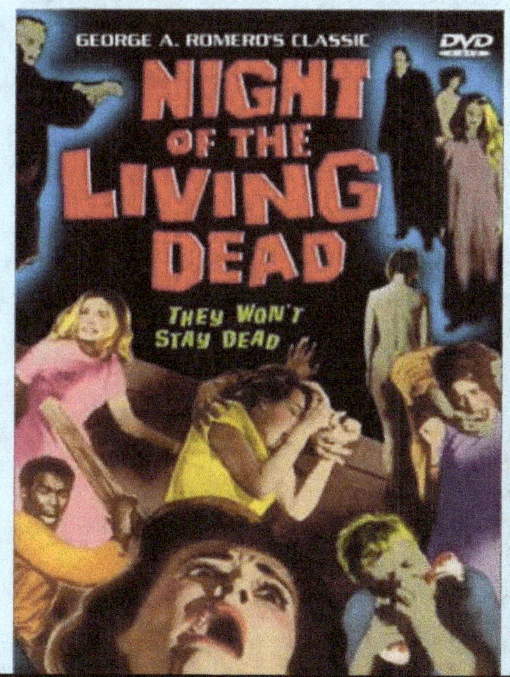

Dark Riddle

LDP: Please tell us a little bit about yourself and how you came to be a writer.

AP: Well, I'm a writer/publisher based in Winnipeg, MB, Canada. I run a company called Coscom Entertainment, which specializes in monster and superhero fiction. I've been writing seriously since 2000 and have been in the publishing game in one way or another since 2003. Though Coscom Entertainment was an idea of mine since way back in high school, it made its debut on the market in 2004 despite my registering the business back in 2001. Recently, it's grown to be a company with reprint deals in New York and also film representation in LA.

LDP: What is the title of your book(s)?

AP: I've written a ton of books, ranging from horror, to fantasy to superhero, Christian fiction, poetry and more. The most recent ones zombie-wise have been: Blood of the Dead (Undead World Trilogy, Book One), Possession of the Dead (Undead World Trilogy, Book Two), and Zombie Fight Night: Battles of the Dead. I also run a free zombie serial novel on my website, www.canisterx.com, called Zomtropolis, with new installments published for free every Friday. On the superhero front, my character, Axiom-man (a kind of hybrid of Superman, Spider-Man and Batman), has appeared in four novels, one short story and one comic thus far. They are: Axiom-man, First Night Out, Doorway of Darkness, The Dead Land, Black Water and Of Magic and Men. On the horror front, my most recent is my first short story collection, Magic Man Plus 15 Tales of Terror, which gathers my best short fiction spanning a decade. All of these are available in paperback and eBook format on Amazon.com or at your favorite online retailer, and also through your local bookstore.

LDP: What are the book(s) about?

AP: The Undead World Trilogy (Blood of the Dead, Possession of the Dead, and the forthcoming third book) is about survival during a zombie apocalypse, and follows the main character of Joe Bailey, who's a self-appointed zombie hunter after witnessing the death/ undeath of the love of his life, April. It's a story about love, redemption, and, of course, good old-fashioned shoot 'em up zombie horror. It's also unlike any other zombie series out there, so far as I'm aware, as it contains a supernatural element, time travel, and zombies that stand over fifteen-stories high. Zombie Fight Night is like Mortal Kombat meets your favorite monster flick. It's about a guy named Mick, who lost a load of cash betting on

UFC-style zombie fights where—as a means for humanity to take revenge on the dead after all they stole from us—the undead fight iconic monsters like werewolves and vampires, and martial arts experts like ninjas and samurai. Axiom-man also makes an appearance as one of the fighters, likewise a robot and Bruce Lee, plus a bunch of others. Aside from the fighting, the premise is Mick needs to bet huge and big to dig himself out of the financial hole he's in and not get killed by the loan sharks that want him dead. My Axiom-man series—official name: The Axiom-man Saga—is about a young guy named Gabriel Garrison, who one night was bestowed great power by a nameless messenger but without explanation or even direction as to what to do with it. It follows his journey of deciding to put his powers to good use, becoming a superhero, and more importantly, asks the question that if a super-powered superhero showed up in our world tomorrow, how would that realistically pan out? My thought has always been that they suddenly wouldn't find themselves neck deep in a world of supervillains, but would instead start out doing small stuff like stopping muggers, or even Johns transacting with a hooker. And if a villain did show up, they wouldn't suddenly start gunning for the hero because "that's what villains" do, but would instead pursue their own agenda. To make things interesting, however, a villain does show up but the take on it is the villain is tied directly into the hero, two sides of the same coin. What do I mean? Read and find out.

LDP: What do you think people would like about your book/s and why?

AP: I've been told that one of my strengths as a writer is my character development, and though I'll leave that judgment ultimately up to the reader, it is the characters that I'm most interested in crafting when I write a story. I do my best to really put the reader in that person's shoes, share that person's thoughts and feelings, and—hopefully— justify their actions, good or bad, based on "being in those shoes." I'm also a proud fanboy and love all things pop culture. That passion shows in my work, especially the superhero stuff. But even looking at the zombie stuff, you can see the mentality of a Good vs. Evil fanatic at work, bringing a mature comic book sensibility to whatever story I'm working on.

LDP: Have you had any other publications? If so, where?

AP: I've always published my novels independently by choice, but back when I started in in this game, I sold a bunch of short stories and still sell them to this day. I've been in anthologies like Dead Worlds: Undead Stories Vol 1, War Wolves, Light at the Edge of Darkness, The Parasitorium: Parasitic Sands, The Horror Writers' Network Presents: New Voices in Horror, and others.

LDP: What inspires you as a writer?

AP: Numerous things. When I started writing, it was a way to deal with some profound and life-altering heartache. Nowadays, I try and absorb inspiration from wherever I can, whether that's fellow authors, writers I admire, comic creators, business owners, life in general.

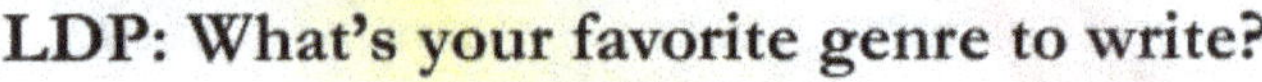

LDP: Who's your favorite author?

I love Terry Goodkind. His Sword of Truth series was a life-changer for me. His prose is crazy descriptive, but in that good way and doesn't bog you down. Stephen King, of course, Alan Moore and Warren Ellis. I also dig guys like Keith Gouveia, Lorne Dixon and Eric S. Brown.

LDP: What's your favorite genre to read?

AP: Comics. Superhero ones, mainly. For books: horror and thriller are the big ones, but I also enjoy love stories, too. Not romance, but love stories, bittersweet ones like The Notebook. I even wrote a love story of my own under the pseudonym Peter Fox. It's called April, and it's available in paperback and eBook.

LDP: What's your favorite genre to write?

AP: Probably horror, though superhero fiction is tied right up there with it. To me, they're pretty much interchangeable because it's all about Good and Evil. The only difference is in one genre they wear costumes, and in the other they don't.

LDP: What advice do you have for writers?

AP: Never give up. I think that's the most important one. Just write, pursue, and go after the craft with abandon. Don't let others get you down. Don't let yourself get you down. Perseverance is everything in this business if you want to get anywhere. Sure, splash-in-the-pan successes happen, but most writers have to work like dogs to make it. And never pay to be published. Ever. Period.

LDP: Of all the characters in your story, which is your favorite and why?

AP: Axiom-man. Easy. It's a superhero fantasy I've had since I was kid that is now being committed to paper. The character deals with a lot of stuff I've been through, thoughts and feelings I've experienced, as well he's a means for me to explore the superhero genre and the themes and ideas within it that I've always cherished.

LDP: Have you ever co-written anything with another author? If so, was it a pleasant experience?

AP: Yes. I've written a couple horror and Halloween novellas with Keith Gouveia. One was Devil's Playground, in which he wrote part one of the story and I wrote the second. The other is On Hell's Wings, in which, inspired by a review we got on Devil's Playground, we attempted to write the story with one voice. I had a blast doing it, both writing with someone and working with Keith particularly. He and I see eye-to-eye on many things and have similar backgrounds in this business.

LDP: Of everything you've ever written, what was your favorite?

AP: In terms of fandom-type stuff—and I'm only choosing because you're making me; who can choose their favorite amongst their kids? —my Axiom-man series, my Undead World Trilogy and my limited edition fantasy hardcover, The Way of the Fog. In terms of fiction in general, my love story, April. It's insanely personal to me.

LDP: Do you have any tips on editing that you would like to share?

AP:Do at least three drafts. Wait at least a month between your first and second drafts so you can come at the thing with fresh eyes. I find that changing the font between drafts seems to magnify any typos, which is a good thing. It's a trick I stumbled upon by accident.

LDP: What are your pet peeves or 'issues' with grammar?

AP: Adverbs. I hate them. They turn what could be mature prose into something that sounds juvenile because a lot of kids' books use adverbs to the nines. Point-of-view switches during a scene. If you're going to change character point-of-views, you need to break it up with asterisks.

LDP: Laptop or desktop computer? Which do you prefer?

AP: For writing—a laptop. I like being able to write wherever, whenever.
For book production, desktop. Bigger monitor, my desktop is more powerful than my laptop, and it's also my main Net connection.

LDP: Do you listen to music while you write? If so, what?

AP: Used to be one CD equaled one writing session.
For the past few years, I don't write with music. Don't know how or why I switched. Just did.
Right now I'm just enjoying focusing on my stories without anything else to possibly distract me.

LDP: What time of day do you write?

AP: Book production and business stuff during the day; creative writing time late evening or during the night.

LDP: Are you an 'in the zone' writer, or one that can sit down and write whenever you want?

AP: Pretty much. As long as my brain isn't foggy from fatigue, I can pretty much sit down and go. I get lost in the prose pretty quick and feel that jarring sensation in my chest when something pulls me out.

LDP: Is there anything I didn't ask about that you would like to share with us? Any plugs?

AP: A friendly reminder to check out my website, www.canisterx.com. I blog daily and update my free zombie serial novel, Zomtropolis, every Friday. Also be sure to follow me on Twitter at www.twitter.com/ap_fuchs as I tend to yap on their quite a bit.
And, of course, check into Coscom Entertainment's zombie, monster and superhero book catalog. I'm really proud of the work we've done and can safely say you'll find stuff in our catalog unlike anything else out there. Head on over to www.coscomentertainment.com to see what I mean.

LDP: Thanks for sharing! Best of luck with all your books!

AP: Thank you.

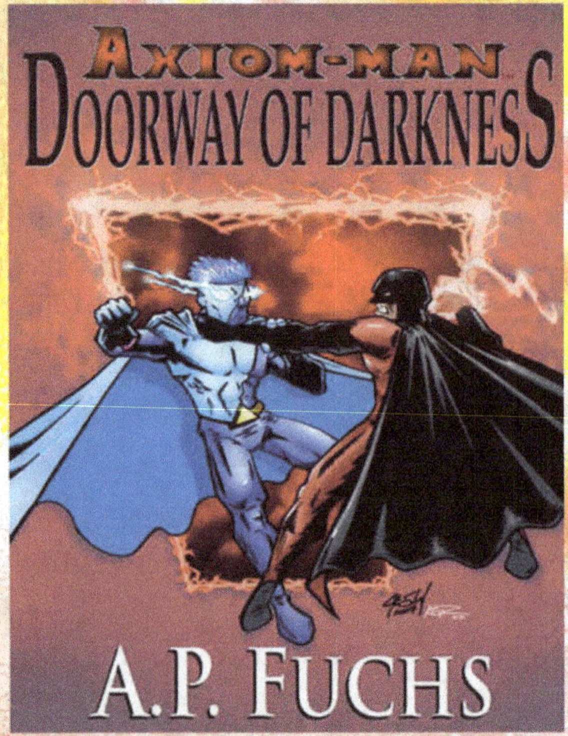

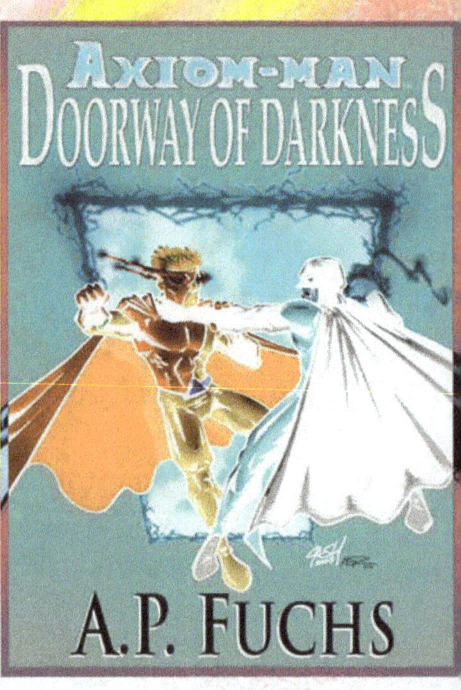

Lenny Wilcox was sure Bob Newbryer, the new real estate agent in Cremwood, was the person responsible for his father's disappearance; at least that's what the local newspaper referred to it as, but Lenny knew his father was dead. Cremwood, population slightly over two-thousand people, was a small farming town located in upstate New York's Adirondack region, ninety minutes north of Lake George. The Cremwood Press was the town's local newspaper, filled with articles pertaining to local fairs; first prizes for things like best pie, politics, and of course who had been thrown in jail for fighting at one of the many drinking holes. These were the types of stories that everyone would know about whether there was a newspaper or not, but it helped with quelling rumors. Weehawkers, a machine parts factory, supported the town, paying half of the population's salaries. When not at work, most of the town's residents spent time at one of the local pubs, playing pool and drinking cold beers. For people who wanted to eat out— escaping the confines of their own kitchens—Gildred's Restaurant served the little community for breakfast, lunch, and dinner. Cremwood was small, but it had everything it needed and everything it ever would, except a real estate agent. Doug Folery, an agent from West Mayville, would shoot over whenever someone needed to sell their home, which wasn't often. When Bob Newbryer moved into town and opened up shop, many folks thought he was crazy, until people started selling. Lenny wondered about the others that had apparently disappeared or moved out since Newbryer's arrival. He was done with college for the semester and could now spend the summer concentrating on his father's disappearance. There had been three disappearances since Newbryer's arrival, along with four families that had moved out of town, leaving their houses on the market for Mr. Newbryer to sell. Lenny had never given it much thought until the day his father went to Newbryer's and never came home. Lenny stayed at school and did some research on Cremwood's real estate man, using one of the college's out-dated library computers. It had been a year since his father vanished. Since then, two more families had moved out of town. He kept in constant touch with his mother and sister, making sure they were all right and not in the mood to sell. He never believed his father had wanted to put the house on the market and he still didn't. Lenny's mother had said he was only going to see what the land was worth and never had any intention of selling. The sheriff and his deputy did an investigation, and from what Lenny understood, were still investigating, if that's what it's called when a case goes unsolved. After a few hours of searching the internet, Lenny found a small piece of information. Newbryer's last place of residence on record was a small town in Minnesota called Gleeville, a mirror image of Cremwood. It had no real estate agent until Newbryer arrived in June of 1989. He stayed there

until June of 1992. It was the only record Lenny could find. Lenny went back to his dorm room after a quick meal in the dining hall, and before leaving campus for summer break, he called the sheriff's office in Gleeville.

"Sheriff's office, Barney speaking," the voice said. "Hello, my name's Lenny Wilcox and I'm doing research on small town disappearances. I was wondering if I could ask you or someone who was there between 1989 and 1992, a few questions." "Hold on just a sec," the man said. Lenny heard a clunk as the phone hit what he guessed was a desktop. He thought he might have to schedule a call-back time, if anyone would even assist him, but another officer picked up. "Hello, this is Sheriff Huff, my deputy informed me you're doing a paper on missing people, is that right?" "Yes, Sheriff, for my school paper," Lenny said surprised. He readied his pen and paper on his knee as he sat on the edge of his mattress. "I don't know how much I can help you, but I'll try. You got me for a few minutes, so shoot," Sheriff Huff said. Lenny was shocked at how easy this was going and got right to the point. "Could you tell me a little starting from 1989? I read that's about the time when the disappearances began." There was a short pause on the other end before the sheriff began speaking. "I remember that time period well. I was a deputy. By the way, do you need my full name or is Sheriff enough?" "No, Sheriff Huff will be fine," Lenny said before adding, "I may not even use your name, but may I if I need to?" "Sure, as long as you write down what I say and don't write down what I ask you not to say." Lenny was caught off guard for a moment, shifting uncomfortably on his hard mattress. Not sure how to respond to Sheriff Huff's statement, he asked, "What do you mean by that, Sheriff?" "Let's just say I'll give you the official story of what went on here. The real story, well, I'll tell you, but I'll deny any truth to it if you put my name to print." Lenny was overrun with excitement but kept his composure. "All right." Sheriff Huff went on to explain how the small town of Gleeville got its first real estate agent in 1989, well, the first one since the early 1900's. Lenny listened as the sheriff told him that from the day Mr. Newbryer moved into town, Huff had never liked him. "The man seemed as friendly as could be, but there was an unease I felt within my bones when I shook hands with him."

"What was it, exactly?" Lenny asked. "Just a feeling, like I was looking into the eyes of a devil or a demon. The way he shook hands with people, like he was sizing them up—seeing who was fresh and who wasn't. I know it sounds weird, but I'm just telling you what I felt. The emotions we feel aren't always describable, you know." "I understand," Lenny responded, hoping he sounded sincere. "People started disappearing or moving out of the area, leaving their homes in the hands of that Newbryer fellow to sell. These people were poor, so I would always ask where they got the money to move." "Where did they?" "Our friendly Mr. Newbryer gave them a portion of what the house was worth, taking it out of the sale." "That seems almost unbelievable," Lenny said. "Yep. Everyone that disappeared over the course of three years, since Newbryer moved to town, all went to see him. So after the disappearance of Mr. Frambrock—he was the last—me and my chief went over to Newbryer's one day. We talked with him for a while and everything checked out. We had no evidence and he gave no suspicious reasons to arrest him. We verified if he really sold the houses and gave the people their money and that all checked out, too. So it was only the one's that disappeared that we really worried about. We never found any one of them, though." "That's it?" Lenny asked. "Nope. Strange thing is when we contacted the families that had moved, they were at least two states away. Now remember, many folks around here grew up in the area and have family, but it didn't seem to matter. And from what I could tell, none of the people that moved out ever came back to visit. We never had any more disappearances and Mr. Newbryer was hardly seen around after that last one. Finally in '92, he sold his business and left. Since we never had anything on him, I couldn't track him and warn the next community he went to." Lenny was silent for a second, allowing all of the sheriff's words to seep in. "So basically, you had your suspicions but nothing ever came of them?" "That's the official story." "Official?" Lenny asked. "Off the record, there's another story. And since I can't tell if you're taping this, you'll have to wait on that." "What? I'm not. We agreed, off the record is off the record," Lenny said, raising his voice. "Sounds like you're a little more than writing a story." The sheriff lowered his voice. "Is he in your town now?" Lenny fell silent as a shiver ran down his spine. The sheriff's words were paralyzing. "How did you know?" "Not too many people would call a small town asking about a specific time period when people started disappearing…for a school paper. And towards the end, you seemed a little too interested. I may be a small town sheriff, but I still have a nose for police work." Lenny should have guessed that might happen, but it didn't matter now as his flesh seemed to gain some heat back. "When can I get the real story?" A dog somewhere in the background of the Gleeville Sheriff's department began barking loudly, making it difficult to hear the conversation. "Look, I have to get going, but give me your address." Lenny gave it to him, and before hanging up, Sheriff Huff had one more thing to say. "Don't do anything until you get the letter from me. You'll have your answers." The phone line went dead. Lenny put the phone back on the base. It was time to head home. He grabbed his suitcases and a few of the items that didn't fit into any bags, and drove home. He arrived home just in time for dinner. His mother and sister had prepared a feast; fresh roasted chicken sautéed in mushroom sauce, freshly cooked carrots, mashed potatoes, corn on the cob so yellow it looked artificial, and homemade buttermilk biscuits. Uncle William and Aunt Peg came over for dinner, making the meal feel more like a small holiday. Lenny told tales of college life, the ones about pulling all-nighters, and when asked about any girlfriends, he told them he had a few and was in no rush to make any commitments. Each member of the family sprinkled in stories of Lenny's father, some bringing laughter, others bringing tears. After dessert, Uncle William and Aunt Peg went home. Lenny and his sister helped their mother clean off the table and began washing the dinner-ware. "Thanks, Mom, dinner was great," Lenny said. "Just what I needed. One can only stomach college food and pizza for so long." "I bet," she answered, sponging a plate clean. "Why? Is college food that bad?" his sister asked, drying off a saucer with the watermelon-decorated dish towels Aunt Peg had gifted them with. "Believe me, Linda, the food isn't that bad and I love pizza, but I need to replenish my body with good, old-fashioned, home cooked meals." "Well, I'm tired of fresh-cooked meals and can't wait to go for pizza." Their town had a local pizza joint, but it just wasn't the same as big city pizza or 'mall pizza,' as Linda liked to call it. Lenny smiled at his sister and even though he couldn't tolerate another slice for at least the remainder of the summer break, he told her he would take her to the Glenn Falls area and get her all the pizza she wanted. "Give me a day or two and we'll go, all right?" he asked. "Okay." "So what are you doing tomorrow?" his mother asked, rinsing the second to last plate in the soapy water. He wasn't sure. He wanted to head over to Newbryer's real estate office and snoop around if the man was out of town, but Sheriff Huff had told him to wait. So what was he going to do? His insides burned with impatience to pay Bob Newbryer a visit. The dinner had been a great distraction and brought him back to a better place than he'd been during the last month. He couldn't wait to get done with college and spend his time figuring out a way to get back at the man who'd stolen his father, and Sheriff Huff's telephone conversation only heightened the anticipation. "Nothing I guess," he said. "Just lie around and catch up on some books I've wanted to read and maybe do some target practice with dad's old guns." His mother paused, the last of the dinner-ware in her hand. "Target practice, since when?" she asked, sounding a little startled, before handing the dish to Linda. "I thought it would be a good idea. I'm not going to shoot any squirrels, just some cans and bottles like me and Dad used to do for fun." Linda had just placed the last dish in the cupboard. She jumped off the counter's ledge where she was sitting. "Ooh, can I come, too?" "No," Lenny said, more harshly than he'd meant. "Fine, you don't have to be so nasty," Linda shot back with a look of disgust on her face. "Sorry, I didn't mean to yell at you, sis," he said. "I'm just tired and I think you need to be a little older. The guns have some kick to them and you'd end up on your rump with a sore shoulder." "Yeah, I think Lenny will do us all a favor if he did his target practice while you were in school," their mother said. Lenny was pleased his mother stepped in, giving her input, and agreeing his sister was too young to be firing guns. It probably wasn't even the guns that Linda cared about as much as spending time with her older brother. After the kitchen was cleaned and all the dishes were put away, Linda went to bed, leaving Lenny and his mom in the living room. "What do you want to do?" he asked her. "I'm paying for all these cable channels, so let's watch a movie. First there's something I want to discuss with you." Lenny had a feeling he knew what it was, he'd heard it before but was always away at school and gathered his mother would sit him down and have the talk with him once he came home for the summer. "Is this about me and the man of the house thing?" he asked, plopping down onto the cushiony sofa. He looked around, noticing all the pictures of family on the walls. Generations of farmers, the land passed down from one to another, like some genetic disposition. "Yes. Please let me finish." She sat in the recliner, her husband's mark worn into the chair's fabric from years of use, like a ghostly impression. "You're the man of this house now. I know you're away at school and all, but you're still the man here now, even more so when you're home." His mother had been sitting up, but nuzzled herself into the chair, as if feeling for her husband's vacant warmth. She pulled on the lever and reclined further as her feet rose, resting on the attached ottoman. "I can get by and do what I must, even during the difficult days, but your sister is young and still growing. I know you're only twenty, but you're all the father your sister has left. She needs you. I need you. Help her; make sure she's all right." Lenny nodded, understanding his role. Needing to lighten the mood, he said, "So you want me to punish her when she's bad?" His mother looked at him, a slight smile spreading over her face. "Very funny

you, but I'm serious about this." "I know." "I'll be there for the normal material—boys, fights, and who knows what—but you'll need to be there for the other stuff. Like drugs, parties and all that kind of teenage activity. She'll come to you about that, not me. I'm just asking for you to be a little more available if she needs you, that's all." Lenny got up, walked over to his mother, and put a hand on her shoulder. "Say no more, I'm already there. I know you worry about us, but we have a good relationship and I'll look out for her and give her all the attention she needs. That goes for you as well. No hiding in your room, crying and keeping it all to yourself. You can talk with me anytime. I know you have Aunt Peg and Aunt Marcy but you have me, too." Lenny saw his mother's eyes fill with tears. He bent down, hugging her and letting her know everything was going to be okay. She patted him on the back after a minute. "Enough of this crying crap. Let's watch a movie or something." She got up and together they sat on the couch. They watched some old movie and ended up going to bed later than normal. In his bed, Lenny laid awake for some time, wondering about what really happened in Minnesota, but knew he would have to wait for the sheriff's letter to get the answers he needed. A few days had gone by and the sheriff's letter still hadn't arrived, but on the fifth day, Lenny's wait ended. He was at the mailbox everyday at one o'clock, the same time the mailman arrived. He grabbed the mail and sifted through it like a money counting machine at the bank. Without having to open any envelopes, he knew which letter was for him. It had no return address and wasn't postmarked from Gleeville, but from some other place he wasn't familiar with. After running into the house and tossing the mail onto the kitchen table—except for his letter—he went upstairs to his bedroom. He sat on his bed, took a deep breath, slid his index finger into the corner of the envelope, and tore the top open. He pulled the letter out and unfolded it.

Dear Mr. Curious,
The man with whom you wish to know about is very dangerous and I ask that you take extreme precautions if and when you deal with him. My associate and I went over to his place of work and investigated. We found nothing. We questioned the man for a good hour, mostly bullshitting about the weather and what not. The bugger didn't bite; he's as cool as ice in a polar bear's fridge. But I did notice something along with my partner. The man in question gave off an eerie feeling, a bad vibe, and the more we stuck around, the worse it got. But the most peculiar thing was the chair that was in front of his desk. When we arrived, a single, red leather chair was before the man's desk, obviously for customers. There were five other chairs in the room, but they were of the metal folding kind. We seemed to have startled him when we entered. The man jumped up, greeted us and moved quickly from behind his desk. He grabbed the chair and pushed it back to where he was sitting and grabbed two of the folding chairs that were against the wall. During our conversation, I stood up and walked as

close as I could to that chair, and he grew very nervous. I even asked if it was an antique and he told me it was. I asked him if I could sit in it and he told me I couldn't, he said it was very old and needed repairing, that the weight of a person might break it, rip the leather even. An antique dealer was on his way over to give him an estimate that evening. I scanned that chair like it was a bathing suit model and found no blood or hairs or anything that might give me a reason to investigate further. I found zilch. The sheriff thought I was crazy but agreed that something wasn't right about the man. We told him good evening and went back to the police station. After some talking, we decided it would be a good idea to keep an eye on that fellow but he left town the very next day. I never saw him again. I thought he was a ghost or something and figured we must have spooked him and he took off. I notified some other towns about him, but figured he was long gone. Well, friend, that's my story. I've never believed in monsters or pure evil, but that man was both, I don't doubt that for a second. Be careful and don't go near that chair, and if you get a chance, burn the damn thing, because that's what I believe it is…damned.

There was no name at the bottom. Lenny couldn't believe what he'd just read. It went far beyond what he thought the sheriff would say. Maybe the man was a serial killer or a thief, but a supernatural chair and an evil man was more than he was ready to believe. It must be true though, why else would the sheriff tell him the story and make it quite clear he didn't want anyone knowing it was from him. Lenny thought long and hard about the correspondence and decided he would pay Mr. Real Estate a visit. The next day Lenny was on his front porch, sitting in the wooden rocker his father had built. He rocked back and forth, casually, wondering what would be the best way to approach Newbryer. Lenny knew the man left his business once a week for an entire day. It was difficult keeping secrets in small towns. Everyone knew everyone's business. Newbryer's affairs, however, weren't well known. He smiled and said hello to those he passed on the street, but never stopped for conversation, as if he were always too busy. He kept a strange schedule, closing his store and leaving a sign indicating the office was closed and would re-open nine a.m. the following day. The particular day off was never the same week to week and never on Sunday. Lenny's impatience crept over him like a high fever. He had to get into Newbryer's place. He began taking walks into town everyday, checking on Newbryer Realty. There had to be a pattern. When Friday arrived, Lenny took his usual walk to town, noticing Newbryer's car wasn't in the driveway. He went into Beth's Wine and Liquor, and asked if Mr. Newbryer was seen leaving town. "Yes, he sure did leave, and in a hurry, too," Beth said, grabbing her pearl necklace, squeezing it and looking out of the window. That man scares me Lenny. He's big city type. He doesn't belong here." Lenny, being the only person in the store, had to endure Beth Arndale's blabber mouth. She was harmless, but a chatterbox nonetheless. At seventy-four years old, Beth was at the center of Cremwood's intelligence community, knowing everyone's business except Bob Newbryer's and that was reason enough for her not to like him. "I tried being friendly to him," she said. "I brought him cookies, tried saying hello a bunch of times, but he just does the same damn thing every time. He acts like he's just so busy. He's polite and all, but it's all hogwash I tell you." She slammed her wrinkly, age-spotted hand down on the counter top. Lenny wanted to break out laughing but reminded himself why he was there and squelched the urge. "Just asking is all, didn't want to get you upset, Mrs. Arndale," he said. He leaned over the counter, gently patting her arm. "Strange, you being right across the street and him being so distant." Lenny had all the information he needed and couldn't wait to get over to the real estate office. "Right you are," she said, before changing the topic. Then she went on about how Marge Sweetwater's kids were wild and out of control, and how Mr. Knowlson always put his trash out a day before he was supposed to, and tons of other gossip, before finally asking him why he came by in the first place. Lenny, caught off guard, quickly responded, "Need some vodka for a dinner party my mom is having." He smiled, trying to appear genuine. "Oh, isn't that sweet. I've always liked your mother, she's a wonderful lady and I give her such credit for all she's done with you kids. She's a strong woman to have gone through what she went through, keeping you and your sister on the right track." And there it was, Lenny thought, another way to keep the conversation going. It wasn't like a day went by he didn't think about his father, but now wasn't the time. "Mrs. Arndale I have to go, I'm sorry. My father was a great man and I'll be sure to tell my mom you thought about her." Lenny asked himself if the lady ever visited or called or brought over cookies, but it didn't matter. There were friends on different levels during times of crisis. Mrs. Arndale was simply an outsider. Lenny walked back to the vodka section and picked up a bottle of Fleischman's. In college it didn't matter what the brand was as long as it did the job, but since he was home and forced into buying a bottle, he would get the good stuff. After purchasing it, he promptly said goodbye and exited the store, realizing he hadn't been asked for I.D. With a bottle of liquor in his right hand, brown-bagged, Lenny walked across the street to Colburt Market. Colburt's was Cremwood's biggest supermarket. It was a bit smaller than a national chain store, but carried everything a grocery store was supposed to carry. The only competing section was the beer aisle, holding as many if not more brands than most other grocery stores. Newbryer's real estate office stood off to the right of Colburt Market. Lenny walked around the left side of the market and went around back.

He worked his way along the dingy cinder block wall, passing the docking stall, making sure no one saw him. He tossed the bottle of vodka into the woods as he neared the end of the building, wishing he'd bought the cheap stuff. Maybe he'd come back for it later. Glancing around the corner, he saw that the coast was clear. He darted across the fifty feet of lawn separating the two properties. Huffing and puffing, he finally made it to the rear of the real estate office, a two hundred year old colonial. He stayed out of sight from the neighboring parking lot and road out front. If anyone came out the back of Colburt's, he'd be seen if they looked his way. He quickly vanquished the thought, knowing he couldn't turn back. Taking a few breaths, trying to get his heart rate lowered, he looked in one of the windows. The amount of caked-on grime made it nearly impossible for him to see inside. Upon closer examination, he realized the shades were drawn. He tried the next window, finding no shade—the window spotlessly clear. Why would one be clean and the other filthy? The man was growing stranger by the moment. Lenny peered in, cupping his hands against the window to block the sun's glare. There were a couple of folding chairs against the far wall and some plaques hanging above them. Most of the room was shrouded in darkness, as if the outside light wasn't allowed in. An uneasiness, like being watched, began to sink in. Fighting against his apprehension, he tried lifting the window. It wouldn't budge. He tried the grubby window, too, drawing the same result. Lenny leaned against the house, sliding down to a sitting position. The mission proved more difficult than expected. Newbryer wasn't a typical town resident. He kept his doors and windows tightly secured like he kept his person. He was 'big city' just as Beth Arndale had said. Frustrated and desperate, seeing his father's warm face in his mind, Lenny sprang to his feet. He picked up a golf ball sized stone and hurled it at the clear window. The stone struck the window with a loud whack, before harmlessly bouncing off as if it was made of crumpled paper. His lips tightened, his eyes becoming narrow slits. Fury seethed from his expanding nostrils like a bull about to charge. Picking up a larger stone, softball size this time, he heaved it at the window with all the strength he could muster. The large stone thudded against the window before dropping heavily to the ground. Dumbfounded, he walked up to the window and struck it with the base of his palm. It was solid, like steel. No, like bullet-proof glass. His anger dissipated like air out of an untied balloon and for the first time he was afraid. The sheriff's letter popped into his mind, giving him the clarity he needed. Newbryer wasn't normal. Regular folks that sold real estate didn't use bullet-proof windows. He'd had enough. He needed to go back to the drawing board and figure out what to do next. He went home and thought about what had transpired. He sat frustrated in his room, trying to figure out what to do next. The man was a mystery and with the security precautions Newbryer took, he wondered if he'd ever find out anything. He went to the front porch to sit and relax. Just as he sat down, Linda's school bus rolled to a stop at the end of their driveway. Seeing her get off and stroll up the driveway, slow motion-like, made him realize how lucky he was. He still had family members that needed him. He made a quick decision. He put the day's events to rest for the night so he could spend some quality time with his sister. "Did you stay after school today?" he asked as she approached the cobblestone path that led from the driveway to the front steps. "Yeah, I had softball practice," she said, hopping up the stairs. "Scoot over." "I know it's a school night, but do you want to go bowling or something?" "Sure, sounds great, but don't think you're gonna get out of taking me to the mall Saturday," she said and punched him in the arm. "I know, it was my suggestion." After dinner, Lenny and Linda went to Cremwood Lanes. They got sodas, ice cream sundaes, and bowled eight games each. Lenny averaged a 204, losing to his sister by ten pins. She had improved since he was away at school and not just at bowling. She had matured. He hated not being able to be around for her, but finishing college was the best thing he could do for her and his mother. "We're going to have a lot of fun this summer," he told her during the car ride home, wanting to assure her that he'd be around. "I know," she said, turning the radio up. Brother and sister sang together, reminding him of when they were both kids, and before the death of their father. They rolled into the driveway shortly after ten, late for a school night, but he'd take any heat his mother gave them. Linda got out first, the plethora of soda running through her like kids in a toy store. Lenny shut off the car and opened the door. He got out and looked up to where the stars were gleaming. It was a beautiful summer night. A gentle breeze blew, seeming to wipe his troubles away like magic. He felt at ease for the first time since coming home. He walked through the front entranceway, letting the screen door slam behind him. His mother wasn't waiting at the door with piercing eyes and a killer stare for keeping Linda out late. A far more dreadful discovery was made when Lenny entered the living room. His mother was standing in front of the sofa, an angry scowl on her face. A man sat in his father's recliner, but his back was to Lenny. "I believe you know Mr. Newbryer," his mother said. The man spun around, a knowing grin plastered across his face. Lenny almost fell over. His heart pounded against his breastbone as if knocking to be let out. "What's he doing here?" "Exactly. You're in a lot of trouble, mister," his mother said. "Lenny," Mr. Newbryer began, "I know your mother is upset, even more so than I am, but please have a seat. I would like you to take a look at something." He motioned for Lenny to sit on the couch. Lenny glanced up at his mother and she looked away, ashamed. He walked around the back of the couch, taking the long route and staying as far away from the real estate man as possible. As he sat down, his mother turned on the television. She pressed play on the remote control. An image came into view like a letterboxed film, but the black bars were on all sides of the screen. A bright glow emitted from a rectangular shape in the middle of the dark area. Lenny could see what the picture was, a window. He saw grass and part of a tree. The image was tranquil until he saw himself. His face matched the red beets in his mom's kitchen. Lenny realized the bastard had a video camera and had taped him trying to break the window of his office. Lenny saw himself looking into the window and trying to open it. He then saw himself leave the camera's view only to return and throw a rock at the glass. He disappeared again from the picture before returning with and throwing a larger rock at the window. His mother hit the pause button, leaving the image of Lenny's angry face on display. His mother began speaking again, but Lenny didn't hear a word. The awkwardness was too much, causing him to retreat into himself like a flower at night. Since coming home from the bowling alley, his good time had taken a nightmarish turn. His mother continued speaking, but he needed time to absorb what had unfolded. Mr. Newbryer was sitting in his father's chair, appearing quite comfortable. The man's shoulders slouched, his body relaxed, but his eyes, like a tiger stalking its prey, pierced Lenny's soul. "Lenny, I'm talking to you," his mother demanded. "Yeah," he said, coming out of his daze. "What were you thinking, trying to break Mr. Newbryer's window?" Lenny took his gaze off the paused image and looked up at her. His eyes met hers and he saw sadness in them. "I'm sorry, Mom…I don't…know." What could he say? Nothing he said would excuse what the video showed, and if he told the truth, his mother would think he was crazy. "I believe the boy was just frustrated and didn't realize what he was doing," Mr. Newbryer said as he sat up straight, elbows on his knees. "Lots of young kids get carried away, especially after going through difficult times." Lenny couldn't believe what the man had said, referring to his father. He felt animalistic, wanting to pounce on Newbryer and beat the evil man to death. He looked to his mother for support. "Is that true?" his mother asked, looking concerned. Lenny decided to go with his father's killer's story. "I guess…I try not to show it around you and Linda. I don't want to upset you two." He couldn't believe how easy the lie came, but it wouldn't have been so easy if the stranger in his dad's seat hadn't spoken first. "Well, we'll deal with that later. I think you owe Mr. Newbryer an apology." Lenny looked Mr. Newbryer in the eyes. "I'm sorry," he said, hoping to sound sincere.

"Thank you and I accept. Luckily there was no damage." The man clapped his hands together, creating a thunderous slap, deafening the room. "Mr. Newbryer, I'm really sorry that you had to come down here so late. I hope we can resolve this without involving the authorities." Mr. Newbryer chuckled, his laugh a deep reverberation. "Calling the authorities is completely unnecessary. We're all allowed to make mistakes. I simply felt you should be informed. That's the only copy," he said, referring to the video, "so do with it as you like." He stood up. "I must be going." "Any coffee or tea before you go? Lenny's mother asked. "No, I must get to bed. I have an early day at the office." Lenny stood up and did something he never thought he could do. He walked over to Mr. Newbryer and put out his hand. "Thank you for being so understanding and not going to the police." He was going to need to scrub his hand clean tonight. "No problem," the man said and shook Lenny's hand. "It's never easy dealing with problems of a serious nature, but when you do it alone it's even harder. Ask your mother for help, she seems like a good woman. Don't keep it all bottled up, it can lead to bad things. I had a good friend in Minnesota. Name was Harold Huff, a sheriff. He had a drinking problem and ran off the road last night. He's alive but in a coma; the doctors don't think he'll come out of it. The sheriff kept things in. I'd hate to see that happen to a nice family like yours." He gave Lenny a wink. Lenny had lost most of the color in his face by the time the story was over. He was trying not to tremble, but he had endured about all he could for the night. He forced a smile, thanking the man again, and knowing a great predator like Newbryer wasn't easily fooled. Lenny went upstairs after saying good night and splashed his face with cold water, washing away a little of the fog that had encompassed his brain. How did Newbryer get to his house? He couldn't remember seeing a car in the driveway and a black Mercedes was hard to overlook. Fearing his mom was going to drive Newbryer home, he ran down the stairs to find his mother doing dishes in the kitchen. Confused, he ran over to the screen door to see Newbryer pulling out of the driveway in his black Mercedes. Lenny ran up the stairs and burst into his sister's room. "Hey, where's the fire? We knock around here," she said. Breathing hard from running up and down the stairs, he asked, "Was there a car in the driveway when we came home?" "No, why?" Linda said, her attention on her homework. "Then how did Mr. Newbryer get here? I saw him pull out just a minute ago." Linda stopped writing and looked up at her brother. "I don't know, maybe he parked on the grass." "Why would he do that?" "So you wouldn't see his car and take off. I heard the whole conversation and just came in here after he left. I'm not stupid, you know. You're really lucky he didn't call the cops." "Do your homework," he began. "Actually, go to bed, it's late." Before his sister could respond, he closed her door and went to his room. He wouldn't get a good night's sleep until he found the truth. Grabbing a flashlight from his

junk drawer, he ran outside and searched the grass next to the driveway, but found no tire impressions. He was certain there had been no car in the driveway or on the grass, and that Mr. Newbryer was no ordinary person. Lenny rolled out of bed a quarter past twelve the next day. He was up until about 5 a.m. when he passed out from sheer exhaustion. He took a shower and went downstairs to eat. While eating his breakfast—two scrambled eggs, toast with cream cheese and a glass of orange juice—he realized he had to approach Mr. Newbryer head on. The man was evil and now Lenny and his family were on his watch list. Lenny was disappointed that he'd allowed himself to get caught and angry now that his family was involved. There was no way he could have predicted that the man's office had a surveillance system. He had to start doing things correctly—like head over to Mr. Newbryer's office and catch the evil bastard off guard. Grabbing a roll of duct tape and his father's 92 FS Beretta—making sure it was loaded—he stuffed the items into his coat pockets. He drove to Colburt Market and parked in the almost deserted lot. A boy collecting shopping carts was walking around, listening to an MP3 player. In small towns everyone noticed everything, but at the same time, there were never enough people around to get an audience. Lenny got out of the car and walked directly over to Mr. Newbryer's place. Anticipation and anxiety grew with every step, and his palms and neckline grew sweaty. He stopped twice, wondering if he should leave and forget the whole thing. He thought about getting liquored up with a bottle of vodka, but the notion was quickly extinguished by the thought of his sister suffering at the hands of Newbryer. Besides, he needed to be clear headed and steady. He shoved his fearful emotions deep down into his soul, the act leaving him bitter. It was a feeling he'd never truly felt before. He kept telling himself he was a warrior, a man, a protector. Occasionally the law found its way into his head, but the law wasn't always right and shouldn't be feared when truth needed to be found. The law was pliable, often changing throughout history, implying that the law was nowhere near perfect. Sometimes people needed to go outside of it. Lenny wasn't planning on killing Newbryer outright, he wanted answers. Answers to the man's purpose. He had always held some belief in the supernatural, even the possibility of aliens, but Mr. Newbryer gave him no doubt that evil was real. The building was a large white colonial built in the late 1800's. It had black shutters on each of the eight windows; the shades were drawn. A wide porch spilled outwards, wrapping around the front and sides of the structure. The building looked warm and friendly, but to Lenny it was an illusion, like a beautiful succubus luring prey. A four stepped staircase gapped the break in the banister and lay outwardly welcoming to business' guests like a tongue welcomes food. Lenny approached Newbryer Realty with caution, taking small, but surefooted, strides. He reached the stairs, counting them as he climbed, unaware of why he was doing it. At the top step, he stopped wishing there were more stairs to count before continuing toward the front door. He stopped again at the door, clearing his mind of any doubt. He had nothing but the desire to see the mission through. Reaching out with his right hand, he grabbed the doorknob and turned. The door opened. He practically tip-toed inside, making sure the door closed behind him without any loud clicks or bangs. He expected a secretary, some demon maybe masked as a person, but there was no one. The converted house-office was as quiet as a funeral home. A waiting room was off to the left of the entrance, with four chairs and art work on the walls. One painting had black crows flying over a town, another had lions biting each other on the neck, and the third had snakes turning into lizards. To the right of the main entrance was another door, this one padlocked. Lenny walked slowly down the hall, proceeding carefully with each step as if crisp autumn leaves where scattered about the floor. He forgot about the gun in his front pocket until one of the floorboards creaked, startling him. He reached inside his pocket and wrapped his hand around the grip. The gun had to stay concealed, at least until he was ready to use it, after which he would have to get the security tape he knew was recording even now, and destroy it. He was beginning to wonder where Mr. Newbryer was, and why he hadn't appeared to see who was in his office. The hall ended and a large room at the back of the building came into view. He lessened his stride, about to peer into the room, when a voice called out. "Hello?" the voice said. "Hello, Mr. Fields? Is that you?" Lenny froze as if icy water had been splashed over him. His state was hesitant, the silence enveloping him. At the same time, the voice had brought an uncomfortable friendliness with it making, Lenny want to answer. A small flame of fear ignited in his gut. He brought forth an image of his father, an image that carried with it sadness and rage. The coldness he had felt earlier came rushing back, dousing his fear. He strode into the room. "No, it's not Mr. Fields, it's me, Lenny." He saw Mr. Newbryer sitting behind a desk in a large black, executive chair. He wore his usual black suit and candy-apple red tie. The man's hair was slicked back, his face stunned. The glass top of the desk was neat. A pen holder with a few pens protruding from it and a manila folder took up the expansive surface. And then Lenny saw it, the chair Sheriff Huff had warned him about, right in front of Newbryer's desk. It was antique in appearance as if from the Renaissance period, made with heavy oak. The armrests, seat and back cushions were covered with dark, crimson leather. It didn't fit the room's décor and in general, it didn't look to belong anywhere on Earth. Lenny wanted to cry out, knowing that his father had sat in that very seat, but he controlled himself. "Lenny, what a surprise. What can I do for you?" Mr. Newbryer asked politely. Lenny took a few steps into the room, stopping about twelve feet from the man. "I've come to ask you a few questions." Mr. Newbryer shifted in his seat. "I see," he said, a look of deep thought on his face. "Well, I'm expecting a client in a few minutes, could this wait until later or perhaps tomorrow?" "No," Lenny said, staring into the man's eyes. "It can't." "Lenny, I'm going to have to ask you to leave. If you don't, I'll have to call the police. You wouldn't want that, would you?" "No, but neither would you. Want to call him Sheriff Huff? Oh wait, you paid him a visit already." Mr. Newbryer's mouth tightened, and his eyes narrowed. "I'm going to ask you one more time to leave, then I'm not going to be so nice." Mr. Newbryer stood up, all six-feet four inches of him. Lenny saw the situation getting out of hand and pulled the gun from his pocket. His hand trembled, slightly. "Sit down, Mr. Newbryer, before someone gets shot." Mr. Newbryer looked even angrier, but took his seat. "I should have handed you over to the authorities before. I can see you're a dangerous boy." Lenny took a step forward, the barrel of his father's gun pointed at the evil man. He needed to be closer should the need arise to shoot. At twelve feet there stood a chance that he would only wound—maybe even miss—the bastard, giving the man time to react. Lenny moved to within eight feet of Newbryer. Less shooting meant less noise. If his theory was correct, he wouldn't be doing any at all. "Look, Lenny, there's no need for violence. I'm happy to answer any questions you have, just put the gun away and have a seat, please." Mr. Newbryer motioned to the wicked chair. "I have a better idea. Why don't you sit there." Lenny motioned to the seat himself. "Move it!" he shouted. Mr. Newbryer glanced at the chair then back at Lenny. "Lenny, this is ridiculous, take a seat and we can discuss whatever's on your mind." "Get up or I'll…" Lenny began, then decided talk was cheap and fired his dad's gun. The office was spacious, but not large enough to let the sound dissipate into the distance. The shot reverberated off the walls, creating a deafening boom that shook Lenny's insides. The bullet missed Newbryer's head by a few inches, lodging itself in the wall behind him. Mr. Newbryer cringed. "What are you doing? Are you mad?" he screamed. "At the moment, I'm void of all emotion, except hate. I want what I came for… answers." Lenny held still, his ears still ringing from the blast. "Okay, okay," the man said, holding out his hands. "Why did you kill my dad?" "I did no such thing," Mr. Newbryer said, responding as if insulted. He brought his arms down, resting them on the armrests. Lenny pulled the hammer back on the gun, the click echoing in the silence. "You're going to die if I don't get an answer, Mr. Newbryer. I came here to get answers and damn it I want them now!" Mr. Newbryer sat up firmly, taking Lenny aback. The man had feared for his life a few seconds ago and now seemed fearless. "You want to talk about death, young man? I'll give you death, when I rip out your soul." He jumped out of his seat, launching himself toward Lenny. He growled like a crazed animal as he flew through the air. Lenny blinked twice, and in-between blinks, he thought the man had changed into a Bengal tiger. Lenny pulled the trigger, and more deafening shots filled the room as the muzzle flashed again and again, but the man's roaring seemed to overpower the gun's blasts. Before Lenny could do anything else, the large man barreled on top of him, sending them both crashing to the floor. Darkness fell over Lenny. He came to slowly, his head pounding. He felt a small gash on the back of his head and withdrew his fingers to find them glistening with blood. Looking around, he saw Mr. Newbryer huddled next to him, lying in a small pool of blood. Lenny crawled over to him after grabbing the gun that had slid a few feet away. He wasn't sure how many shots he'd managed to get off, but he was sure he had enough remaining. Mr. Newbryer looked dead; his mouth hung and his body was limp. Lenny hobbled over to him and felt for a pulse. The man was alive, his pulse strong. He began to stir, mumbling incoherently. Lenny wondered if the man was really human. Without thinking, he knocked the already incapacitated man on the head with the butt of the gun. There was no time for games, he was here to do a job, find answers if he could; the rest he would have to figure out as the situation unfolded. He shoved the gun into his pocket and grabbed Newbryer under the arms. The two hundred and twenty pound body was heavy, but Lenny was strong enough, and dragged the man to the old leather chair. Staring at it, Lenny's skin grew cold as he felt its wickedness. It seemed to pull at his pant legs and jacket, but when he looked, there was nothing grabbing him. The chair also appeared darker in hue than earlier. He could almost swear it was alive, as if it was angered that its master was in trouble. Was he imagining everything? Or was the chair truly evil? Mr. Newbryer started to stir again, snapping Lenny out of his frozen state. He needed to know the truth and he heaved the man onto the chair. Mr. Newbryer slumped on the chair, his head whipping back, leaving his mouth agape. Lenny ran around to the back of the chair and pulled him further onto it. Now Mr. Newbryer was in a full sitting position. Again, Lenny conked him on the head with the butt of the gun, sending a few spatters of blood about. Lenny swallowed hard in disgust as he saw the raw wound had opened wider. He never would have imagined that he was capable of such vicious behavior before today. His actions frightened him, but he realized they were necessary. In order to deal with Newbryer, he needed to be a little like him, unforgiving, but with his own controlled madness. Reaching into his left pocket, Lenny pulled out the roll of duct tape and began wrapping it around his captive and the chair. He circled the man's entire waist and chest area, using almost the entire roll. "Now we wait," Lenny said. He walked over to Mr. Newbryer's executive chair and sat down. It took almost twenty minutes before Newbryer woke up. The down time of waiting had made Lenny second guess what he was doing, but he quickly squashed it. There was no time for uncertainty now, maybe later. "What happened?" Newbryer asked, sounding disoriented. "Hello there, Mr. Newbryer, now we can get down to business." Lenny didn't get up, he felt in complete control for the first time since arriving. "What have you done, boy?" Mr. Newbryer asked in a weak voice. "I don't have a lot of time, especially if my theory is correct, so I'll ask you a few questions and I better get some answers…no I take that back, all the answers." Lenny stood up and proceeded to walk around the desk, making sure to keep a few feet away from the chair and its occupant. "Lenny, you're a very disturbed young man, please, untie me before this gets serious." Lenny stopped walking. This man was incredible. He hadn't thought it was serious yet? The situation, the gunshot wounds, the gashes on his head, and the possible concussion wasn't enough? Lenny didn't have time to think, the man was either bluffing or had been through far worse than this before. "You don't think this is serious yet?" Lenny asked. "I think it's deadly serious, but I must say it could be a lot worse. I don't want to see you throw your life away by killing me. What would your mother do then? Or your sister?" He turned his head from left to right as if trying to get out a kink. "Why are you abducting people?" Lenny asked and began walking around the room again. Where do you take them?" "I don't know what you're talking about, so would you please stop this madness and untie me." He showed a tinge of anger then and Lenny wondered if the man was indeed afraid. "Am I merely just a boy to you?" Lenny asked. "Yes, you're a confused and angry boy. I can be quite sympathetic to that, so you have nothing to fear from me or the authorities. That is, if you stop this now." Lenny walked in front of Mr. Newbryer and pulled the gun from his pocket. "See this, I don't need this. I know it doesn't frighten you. I've seen the way you look at me, like I was prey." He put the gun down on the desk, and walked back around and sat in the executive chair. "I've got longer than you, and you know it. So you better start talking." "I'll not say another word to you." Newbryer seemed out of sorts with that last word, and Lenny wondered how long he had before it would be too late. A few minutes had gone by and Lenny kept repeating the same questions. "Where do you take the people and why do you do it?" Newbryer hadn't said a peep. An hour went by and Lenny kept repeating himself. He began to think the situation was hopeless, that the man

would never talk. He couldn't stop asking, or doubt might seek in. The fight against evil wasn't going to be easy and he was determined to win. The time was creeping upon eleven in the evening. when the man spoke. "All right, I'll talk, but you have to let me have some water first, my mouth is dry." Lenny couldn't believe it, but it was a start. He ran down the hall to the waiting room and grabbed Newbryer a cup of water from the water cooler. On his way back, he began to worry if this was a trick and that Newbryer had somehow slid out of his bonds. Lenny drew the gun and approached the room with the hesitation of a rabbit coming out of its hole during hunting season. He peered around the doorway and saw that everything was the same as it was when he'd left the room. "Please, a little in my mouth, but pour the rest over my head, please. I'm very hot." Lenny thought the request an odd one and stopped to think about it. It wasn't warm in the room, but maybe the constant knocks to the head made Newbryer feel hot. Lenny walked over to the bound man and noticed the chair was a lighter shade of burgundy. He was sure of it now, it had changed color. "What are you doing? Give me the water," he growled. Lenny bent down to get a closer view of the chair's material. The eerie feeling he had before was gone, and he sensed anticipation from the chair. He couldn't explain it, but the chair was alive, just as he suspected. Standing back up, Lenny held the cup over the arm of the chair and tilted it. "Stop that now!" Newbryer howled. "On me, pour that fucking water on me, boy!" He was yelling now. Lenny almost smiled with delight at Newbryer's anger, because it was fear, not anger that he was showing. Lenny let a drop of water spill onto the arm of the chair. The area where the drop landed rippled and turned a blackish red. The feeling of anger erupted again, not from Newbryer, but from the chair. Lenny could feel as if the chair was looking at him with cold, angry eyes. The area lightened in color again, but the leather was now cracked, as if it had dried out. Lenny stood up and took a few steps back. "So, the chair is alive," he said, half-heartedly. He stopped and looked directly into Newbryer's eyes. "What are you?" "Boy, I'm your worst nightmare—your fears and everything you despise about humanity. I'll peel the flesh from your bones and feast on your organs. You think you've won, but you're marked now—a dead flesh puppet. You and your whole family are finished. I'm going to eat your souls, devour your essence." His voice had changed, it was lower and almost echoing within itself. "Now let me out of this fucking chair and I'll let them live. You don't have to ruin it for them." He was lurching forward, the duct tape thinned to half its width as he forced his weight on it. So far it held. The gunshot wounds must have weakened him, Lenny thought, otherwise he was sure the tape would've snapped if the man had been at full strength. "You have no authority anymore, you never did, Mr. Newbryer. It was the chair the whole time, not you. You're just a junky, all juiced up on speed. You have no real power here!" Lenny screamed. Lenny turned to leave when Newbryer began screaming. "No, no don't leave me like this! Get me out of this thing's mouth. I beg you, please!" "I know what happened, Mr. Newbryer," Lenny said softly. "It's all over now." "You little bastard. How could you know? I'm not supposed to be dinner…you are!" The man's pupils were the size of pinheads. The tape stretched further and Lenny was about to knock him on his head again, when the entire chair turned blood red. Newbryer seemed to be shrinking. He yelled and tried kicking, but he was disappearing fast. The chair was absorbing him, eating him. He began to look like melted wax, his insides dissolving. His skin went last, but his business suit, underwear and socks stayed untouched. Like a rib bone stripped of all its meat, the clothing was perfectly clean, not so much as a spot of blood left on it. Lenny stood in awe of the event, feeling disgusted but satisfied. The chair was the perfect murdering machine, it left no evidence. It even cleaned the blood from the bullet holes in the suit. After a few minutes, the chair shined and lightened in color again. It looked brand new, and better than when Lenny had seen it earlier. It must be full, Lenny thought. So he'd finally gotten to the truth. He now knew where all the people had gone and why Newbryer was never caught. But Lenny's mission was only half complete. He walked out of the room and down the hallway, returning with an unopened, five gallon water bottle on his shoulder. He walked over to the chair, ripped off the seal, and let the water pour over the old chair. Gallons of fresh spring water splashed everywhere. The chair's color went dark red again, and it seemed to seethe with hate. Lenny almost fell back from its force, but he held strong, letting the water fight his battle. The chair began to rip and crack, and the wooden arms began to splinter, the legs crumbling to dust. The leather tore further, folding in on itself like loose skin. Lenny let the last drops of water tumble to the floor where a handful of gray ash lay. He left the room, returning with another water bottle, pouring more water over the remaining ashes, they soon disappeared. Lenny knew there could be no ashes left, not even a spec. He thought about sneaking out, making sure no one saw him leave, but he decided it didn't matter. There was no evidence except for a few bullets in the walls, and from a casual glance, they looked like someone had simply used a hammer rather messily. A little spackle and the walls would be as good as new Lenny walked home and had dinner with his family. He never told anyone what happened, but always wondered if there were more Mr. Newbryers in the world. After college he became a traveling salesman, to investigate disappearances in small towns, to make

absolutely sure there were no more Mr. Newbryers. He knew that if he ever found one, he would know exactly what to do.

The End

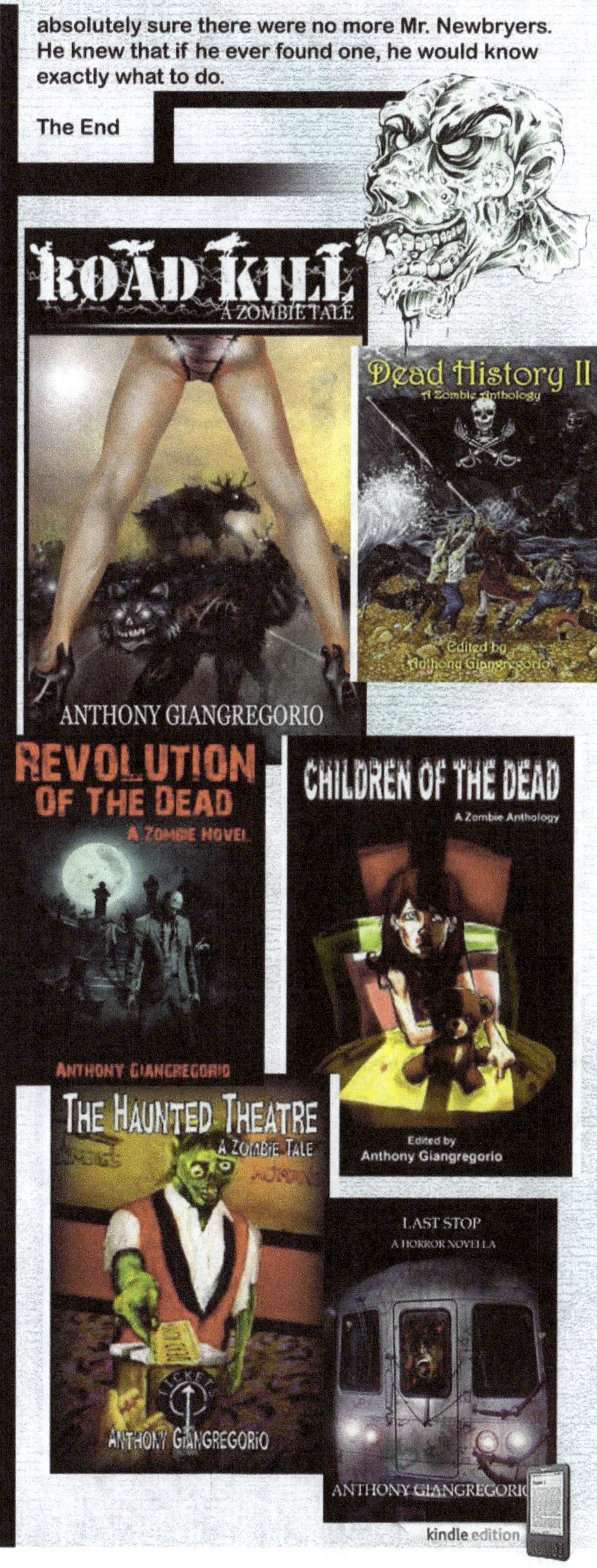

LDP: Can you please introduce yourself?

SF My name is Sarah French and I'm an independent actress and model.

LDP: As a child, did you ever think you would have chosen acting as a career path?

SF Looking back, I always loved performing in front of people or a camera. Even as a kid, I'd put on plays for family members and friends. Performing has always been an interest for me. Never thought I'd be where I am today.

LDP: What inspired you to get into acting?

SF My love for horror films actually inspired me. I started modeling and about six months later, wanted to do more than that, I wanted to be on film with all the other amazing women out there. I wanted to be one of those women that were in horror films and I wanted to at least try it to see if I liked it. I went on a horror forum, found a local film company wanting an actress for a short horror film, and auditioned for it. I got the part and since then, it's all history.

LDP: Were you always attracted to horror themes and films?

SF Since about the age of five, I've always loved horror films. The very first horror film I saw, that I can remember, was 'Childs Play.' That film scared the hell out of me, and I loved horror ever since. I can thank my Grandma for that.

LDP: Modern takes on the notion of so-called Scream Queens have ushered in groups like the Suicide Girls and Sisters of Sin. Do you feel such groups can act as a stepping stone toward getting into films?

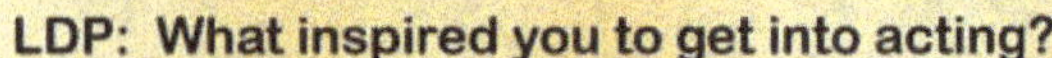

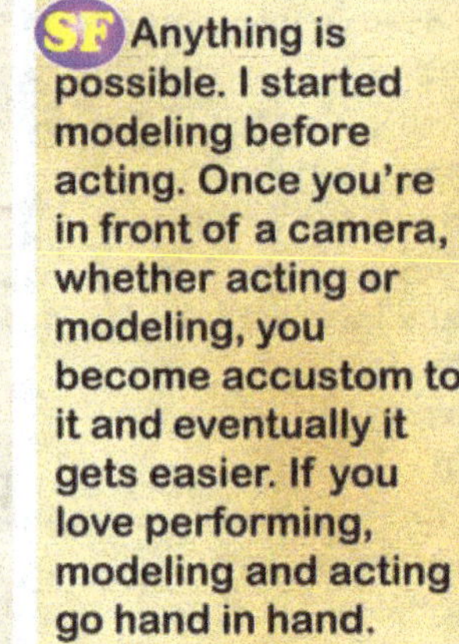

SF Anything is possible. I started modeling before acting. Once you're in front of a camera, whether acting or modeling, you become accustom to it and eventually it gets easier. If you love performing, modeling and acting go hand in hand.

LDP: Name some of your favorite horror & Sci-Fi films?

SF Alien, Predator, original Day and Dawn of the Dead, Pet Cemetery, Child's Play, Jaws, Leprechaun, The Thing, Creepshow, Texas Chainsaw Massacre, Exorcist, Omen, The Shining, Evil Dead, Halloween 2&3, Return of the Living Dead, Friday the 13th series, and Nightmare on Elm Street series. That's good for now.

LDP: Who were some of the people that you were inspired by most as an actress?

SF Cassandra Peterson, Lucy Lawless, and Jamie Lee Curtis to name a few.

LDP: Are you ever squeamish about taking on roles where the special effects might be overtly gruesome?

SF Ha ha, that's a good question. I'm going to be honest about this one. Yes. Some things do gross me out, especially if there's real animal meat and blood involved. But, since I'm getting paid, bring it on!

LDP: Live plays such a Phantom of the Opera rely heavily of horror themes, have you ever acted in a play?

SF I've done small plays here and there for school, but nothing major. I actually really like it. If and when I have more time, I'd love to do another play in the future.

LDP: Is there a certain ritual that you go through to prepare for a part?

SF When I first started in the industry, I'd practice for weeks before filming, day and night nonstop. After a few years, I've learned to take it easy and not to over analyze the script. I like to study a week tops and just let it flow naturally.

LDP: What would be the proverbial perfect-role for you?

SF The perfect role for me would be one where I get to kick some major ass!

LDP: Have you ever considered a role too physical to accept?

SF The more physical, the better. I'll accept any challenge thrown at me... for the right price that is, ha ha. I'm in very good shape.... I work out and eat healthy. Bring it on!

LDP: Out of all your roles in different films, which one was your favorite?

SF I usually get asked to pick a favorite film of mine and that's just not possible. Favorite role, on the other hand, I'd have to say a role I've done where I was the bad guy in the end. In most of my films, I play the innocent one, so it's nice to be the bad guy every now and then. It's nice to step out of your comfort zone to do something new and to me that's what it's all about.

LDP: Is there anything you would like to say to other girls that want to follow your path in acting?

SF I'd say just be careful and smart about things. Use common sense and check your resources. Never do anything you feel uncomfortable about.

LDP: What current projects are you working on, and what could we look forward to from you in the future?

SF I'm currently working on 'Hallow Pointe,' which is in pre-production. We just got a new director, Thomas Churchill, and things are looking great. We're looking to film this summer. Also, I'm doing more and more conventions all around. Keep checking my website for updates.

LDP: How and where can fans contact you for more information on your appearances?

SF They can access my website at 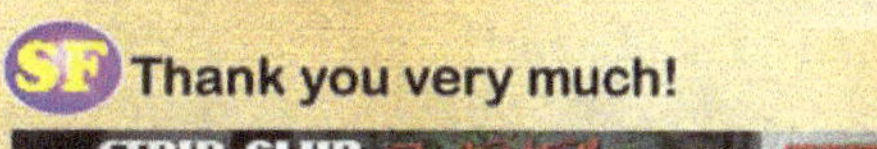 www.scarletsalem.net where they can find my contact info.

LDP: Thank you for taking the time to talk with us, it's been wonderful.

SF Thank you very much!

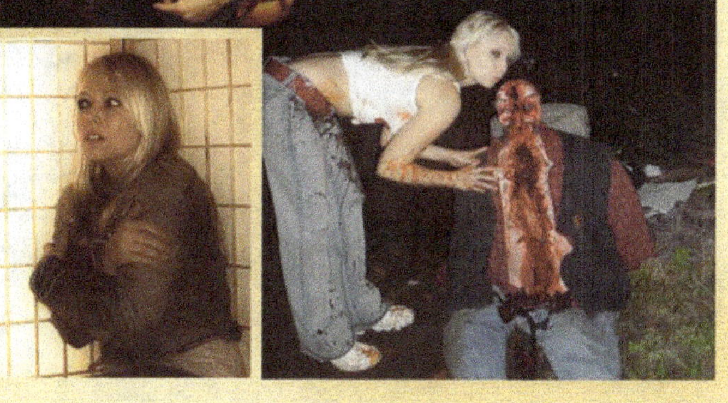

Samhane by Daniel I. Russell
ISBN: 978-0-9824969-8-5
Age Group: Adult

After much waiting and anticipation I finally got to tear into "Samhane," a truly twisted horror story with many faceted aspects to scare your pants off. Daniel I. Russell weaves a tale of horror that isn't afraid to take the step up to extreme, delving into the deepest and darkest of your fears to excite, scare, and disgust you all at once. The sheer brilliance of the mix presses your mind to its limits and holds you at the edge of your seat as you wait to find out what's down the next twisted path. Donald Patterson innocently buys a laptop online and goes to pick it up, since the seller lives close by. He doesn't at the time know of the man—Roger's—twisted, dark secrets. But after returning home and finding a "questionable" video left in the computer, Don begins to wonder about the source of his purchase. Unfortunately, his lack of action leads to his fiancée, Beverly's abduction. He pursues Roger to Samhane, seeking to rescue the woman he loves. Meanwhile… Brian Rathbone and his son, Sam, are stuck in Samhane, dealing with the monsters on the loose that are terrorizing the town. Brian, unsure of what's really going on, tries to keep his mouth shut and pick up his paycheck, putting his life, and his son's, in danger. Will they be able to stop The Order of Zandathru, the God of Chaos? Or will they all die in the twisted confines of the small town of Samhane? Daniel dazzles me with his characterization, which is VERY believable, while at the same time he holds the tension aloft until the very end of the book, keeping the reader with him the entire time. I also admire his strength as a writer to not be afraid to mix in some extreme elements that scare most of us, but we aren't willing to admit openly. While it might disgust you, at the same time, you know you wouldn't want to be in the victim's shoes. I have to rate this book at five out of five stars. You'll want to read it over and over again, enjoying it (shuddering) each and every time.

These Trespasses by Kenneth W. Cain
ISBN: 978-0615444147
Age Group: Adult

Do you like sci-fi mixed in with your horror? Because that's what you're going to get when you read this book. But you won't have to leave the comfort of Earth, because it will all come to you, courtesy of the government! Kenneth W. Cain spins a tale of otherworldly horror for us to delve into, ripping simple people just like us from their simple lives and tossing them to the wolves… er…aliens. Marty gets quite a shock when his brother is bitten by a mosquito; it throws his calm world into a whirlwind of chaos…again. He doesn't know how much he can take, but knows he'll never give up. Sheila reads Marty's note and finds hope – and something more – beyond the world of slaughter around her, and seeks him and his friends out for companionship before she joins the ranks of the dead, or worse! Bernard, a kindly fellow and Marty's right hand man, meets an end he wasn't counting on, but finds a new life that isn't his. Through it all, he finally learns to admit his love for Nancy, but will that be enough? Or will everything fall apart for them both? Sandy and Ike are wild cards at best, but with hidden strengths. Will they bring good or bad to the small band of survivors? Together they battle the aliens among them, seeking to understand and destroy what they can't control, but can easily control them. Can they overcome their fear of being torn apart or captured to do what is needed to save the day? The book was interesting and creative, there's no doubt about that. But, it's clear it's Kenneth W. Cain's first novel. Some areas were unclear as to what was going on and the point of view was confusing, but despite the drawbacks, the story is still there and shines through, and I look forward to reading more of his work in the future. I give this book three out of five stars.

LIVING DEAD PRESS PRESENTS

Film & Book Reviews: Exclusive Author Interviews: Art and Commentary

Reviewed by Rebecca Besser

Alien Siege by David Alan Dickens

ISN: 9781438239422
Age Group: Adult

Aliens are creatures that no matter how much we hear or see about them, it always leaves us wondering. What if they're real? What would they really look like? Would they be friendly or hostile? In this book we find that aliens have been around for a long time – longer than any of us have dreamed, and they are hungry and waiting. David Alan Dickens pushes your mind's limits as ancient gods of past civilizations stalk the present day population, seeking to sate their appetite for human flesh in this fast-paced, exciting ride on the edge of planet Earth. Mark Black becomes frustrated with life and himself when he loses almost everything he has in a game of cards. Now he's just doing his job bulldozing down the Borabi jungle in India, making way for a mega railroad project. But strange mass graves filled with bones and ancient artifacts keep turning up as they excavate the sites, which leads to his meeting Tatiana, a beautiful woman who, through her research, has discovered the unearthly truth. After Mark uncovers a very large, strange container that seems impervious to damage, they call in a specialist to open it with a laser so they can see what's inside. To everyone's shock, when the unit is opened, they find radiation…and alien beings. The military arrives to take control and an alarm goes off while they are harvesting some of the beings for research and it triggers others – who are superior in intellect – who start appearing around the globe. American leaders, as well as others around the world, scrabble to make sense of what's happening and to take action that will protect the people of Earth, but when the aliens use their radiation weaponry, it seems there is no hope for anyone. A fleet of ships departs from a far off galaxy to come to the aid of the vessels humanity has learned to take down, while the fate of the world rests on a shaky plan. Will mankind survive? Or will everyone become victims of the Alien Siege? This book was fun to read and was fast-paced. It was easy for me to pick up and get back into the story. The biggest drawback for me was that there were a lot of characters and with everything moving so fast, you couldn't really get in-depth with any of them, so I give this book a four out five star rating.

Reviewed by Jesus Morales

Damnation Alley by Roger Zelazny

Roger Zelazny wrote Damnation Alley in 1967 as a short science fiction story, which later, he expanded into a full novel in 1969. A film adaptation of the novel version was released in 1977 and gained the book much fame in that era. The 1977 film was loosely based on the original novel and was directed by Jack Smight. Roger Zelazny had liked the original script by Lukas Heller and expected that to be the filmed version. Yet, he didn't realize until he saw it in the theater that the production script was actually done by Alan Sharp and was quite different. Oddly, he said he never liked the movie and was embarrassed by it. That certainly wasn't the case for viewing audiences and even today it's considered an honorable cult classic. Zelazny's book, in the opinion of many, was a quintessential masterpiece of the science fiction genera of that era. More so, today scores of films and video games seem to take a big influence from Roger Zelazny's novel. Films such as Doomsday, Land of the Dead, and the very popular FALLOUT video game series seem to have a great deal of reference to the book, including, radioactive cockroaches, giant scorpions, an armored wasteland vehicle, and a decimated America where environmental hazards reek havoc throughout the country. However, it's often reflected that Zelazny's initial premise for the book might have been overlooked by its rich and fantastical concepts. Damnation Alley is a book about environmental devastation and it's clear that the author wanted to warn people of the very real nuclear threat of the times. In books like McCormick's The Road, a far more subtle and serious take is dished out. Yet, Roger Zelazny's notion of the American wasteland still lives on, through its ominous and possibly prophesied warnings.

PATIENT ZERO BY JONATHAN MAYBERRY

Reviewed by Anthony Giangregorio

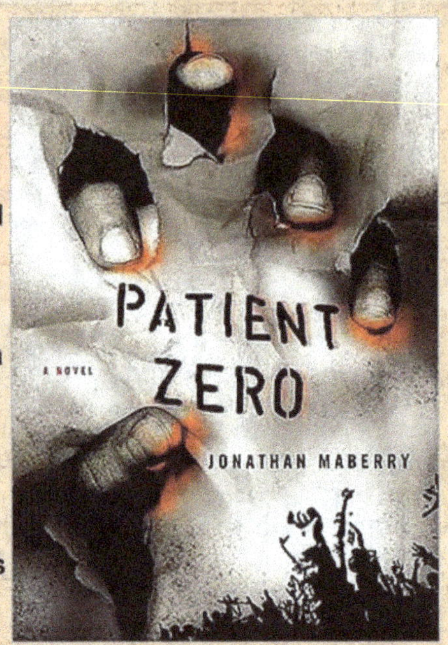

Joe Ledger is a Baltimore detective that finds himself recruited to a task force called the DMS (Department of Military Science), after a raid where the terrorist he shoots doesn't stay down and is in fact a zombie. It seems a terrorist group, funded by some very rich men have managed to create a virus that basically brings the dead back to life. Each strain is worse than the last, and if not stopped, the bioweapon will sweep across the globe, changing every man, woman and child into flesh-eating zombies. The writing is fast and well-paced with humor sprinkled in all the right places. The characters are flawed which makes them all the more believable. Joe is a competent man, a hero, though modest. Most male readers will find themselves wondering what they would do in Joe's shoes. Like a good Ludlum novel, the book is heavy on the whys and hows, and only a few times gets weighed down with what I call 'too much information.' It's great to know how the virus works but those of us who want action don't want to read ten pages about cells and test tubes and other technical jargon that goes right over our heads. Luckily, that's not the case here. Though once or twice the book gets heavy with technical jargon ect, it never goes overboard and no sooner is some scientist done lecturing, then something happens that means bullets are flying and zombies are getting shot. The zombie action is top notch and as I read these scenes I could easily see it playing out as a movie for a summer blockbuster.

Building to a climax as any book should, the finish should leave any reader very satisfied and not wanting in the least, with the exception of wanting to read more of Joe and the DMS, of course. Luckily, there are more books in the series and I'm looking forward to reading each one. So if you're tired of all the self-published dreck that's out there, get this book and see how a zombie novel should truly be done. And it's nice to know the Joes in the world are keeping us safe from zombies and terrorists, and that we get to read about them, too.

NEW FICTION FROM LIVING DEAD PRESS!

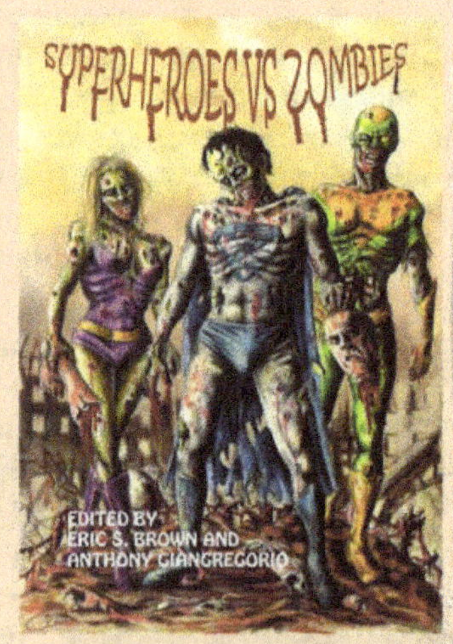

First, I'll start with the novella "Darkness Under the Sun." I really enjoyed this truly creepy tale about innocence meeting evil. And whether you are a fan of Koontz or not, this is a story that any fan of horror will enjoy. I highly recommend grabbing "Darkness Under the Sun" and reading it before the accompanying novel "What the Night Knows."

It isn't necessary, but it will supply the reader with a firsthand look at the antagonist for the novel. Before I begin my review of "What the Night Knows" I have to state, like many others, that I have been disappointed with Dean Koontz' last few titles. His older works were much more engaging, interesting and written as if he loved writing them and didn't just need to put out a book every year. With "What the Night Knows," he has swung back towards his old style, but didn't quite make it back all the way. I found it to be a mixture of new Koontz and old Koontz. "What the Night Knows" is a vicious and wicked supernatural tale about innocence lost, misdirection of parenting and youth, and just plain old evil. The main antagonist in the story is Alton Turner Blackwood, a demented serial killer with a horrific past. This isn't one of those tales where the reader doesn't know a lot about the bad guy. Koontz goes into detail about his character, from boyhood to adulthood. The use of a journal, spread out between chapters from the killer, is fantastic at bringing the character to life; explaining why he is the way he is without shoving it down the reader's throat all at once. The protagonist, John Calvino, is a homicide detective and a person with a devastating past and is directly linked to the killer. Koontz does all this flawlessly and believably. But I found John a little weak and unsure of himself, where as Alton Blackwood was sure of himself and as strong of a character as one gets. It almost felt as if Koontz wanted to write a story about Blackwood, wanting the character to be the focus of the tale instead of the protagonist being at the heart. I don't want to give away too much, but this is a good story about a serial killer coming back from beyond the grave.

I found myself deeply involved in the book, wanting to keep reading until the end—well, almost the end. There were a number of sick baddies in this book to keep the horror fan interested in what each one will do, especially when involved with Blackwood. The main reason the book wasn't one of his best works and was just "good," was the ending. I found it to be quick and pulled-out-of-a-hat, as if Koontz needed to finish it up and didn't know how to end it. It just didn't work for me, though other readers might feel different. There is also something left undone, a real wicked scene, and I'm hoping Koontz will deal with this in another book and has left it open for that very reason. All in all, I recommend any fan of Koontz and supernatural horror to read this book. Though the ending wasn't as strong as some of his other books, it was still an enjoyable read.

"Eating 'em was more fun than blowing their gnarly green heads off. But why dicker when you could do both? The fresher ones were blue. That was important if you wanted to avoid cramps, salmonella. Eat a green one and you'd be yodeling down the big porcelain megaphone in no time."

So begins the classic zombie tale "Jerry's Kids Meet Wormboy." It's hard to believe it's over twenty years since I first read this story. Harder still to believe that other than occasionally stumbling across one of Schow's other stories in an anthology or zine, it's taken me two decades to seek out the author's work. By chance, his recent novel "Internecine" was among the new releases at my local library. The book floored me, and reading it I knew it was one of those rare few I'd have to visit again. In the last couple of months I've been catching up. All I can do is say a big thanks to the librarian who put "Internecine" on display. Without a doubt, Schow consistently delivers what I look for from a writer. Wise, insightful, but not too wise or insightful, not so much he let's it get in the way of his terrific storytelling. Schow's one of those writers who draws you in and traps you, the steel clench jaws of his prose working deep into your bones long after you've turned the last page. "Internecine" (which means conflict on two opposing sides) is the best action thriller Hollywood never made. Think "Fight Club" meets "Face-Off," mixed with every great LA noir ever written. The next book of Schow's I read was "Gun Work." Like "Internecine" this was a crime novel, but before I get to that a few words on how I could be aware of the author and never really read him. Twenty years, and all I'd read of Schow's were a half dozen stories or so. Loved every one of them. Just never made the effort to see what else he'd written. It's kind of sad when this happens. You feel a genuine sense of regret that you let this author or that author, or this band, or film-maker pass you by for so long. I did the same thing with Bill Lustig. Just never got around to watching "Maniac" or "Maniac Cop" or his other movies, until a buddy gave me crap for having never watched either of them, and did me the great courtesy of loaning me both to see what I'd been missing all these years. Bill Lustig is a great genre film-maker. To have discovered him late is of course far better than to never have discovered him at all. But still you want to kick yourself for wasting so much time watching or reading mediocre tripe, when the really good stuff was just sitting there waiting for you all along. One thing I will say is that, unfortunately, none of Schow's books are presently stocked in any of the bricks and mortar bookstores (at least none in my area), meaning libraries or online sources might be your best bet. Bur back to "Gun Work." If movies like 'The Wild Bunch" and "The Usual Suspects" are your thing, you will love this book. "Gun Work" is released through pulp specialists Hard Case Crime, and though many noir elements are in place (kidnappings, double crosses, revenge) this is more like noir if done by John Woo. Some have compared it to the equivalent of reading an action movie, or have called it gun-porn meets torture-porn, but such comparisons do the book a great injustice. Schow's character insight, his astounding eye for detail in creating an all too believable Mexican hellhole called a hostage hotel (where kidnappers are permitted to stash their hostages for a cut of the take) make this a must read for anyone looking to be challenged. And let's not forget Schow's killer prose. "Barney had been cast in the part, no audition, and now the spotlight was on. He flushed the toilet to give himself an entrance cue. It gurgled and tried to back up. The bowl was ringed with brown stains similar to the strata of calcification on the teeth of many Mexican citizens, a fringe benefit of no fluoride. Estrella obviously enjoyed a better dental plan." The third book of Schow's I've read in as many months is a collection of horror stories, titled "Havoc Swims Jaded."Many of the 13 tales contained herein emphasize character based plots that build to a gore-drenched conclusion ("Plot Twist," "Size Nothing," "Frame Shift") or feature lashings of the old ultra-violence right from the get go ('The Absolute Last of the Ultra Spooky, Super Scary Halloween Horror Nights," "The Thing too Hideous to Describe"). While I enjoyed the 'Twilight Zone' vibe of "Plot Twist," or sexual kinkiness of "Size Nothing" and "Frame Shift," it's in the latter two (Absolutely Last..., Thing too Hideous...) where, for my money, Schow shines most as a short story writer. Striking the right balance between horror and humor is never easy, but when an author gets it right, few approaches seem so well suited to the horror fiction short form. It's in stories like these, as in "Wormboy" all those years earlier, where Schow hits the target, giving us gory goodness, virtuoso writing, and well judged satire. The only downside, as is often the case with satire, is a sense of distance from the characters, with the reader observing from above rather than feeling a connection to them. Consequently, there's less at stake, less fear for the protagonist's threatened survival—less realness to the horror.

Fragile by Brandon Cracraft

When I heard the little boy screaming at the top of his lungs, I thought I was having another flashback. I took a moment to remind myself that it was October 30, 1976; a year and a half after 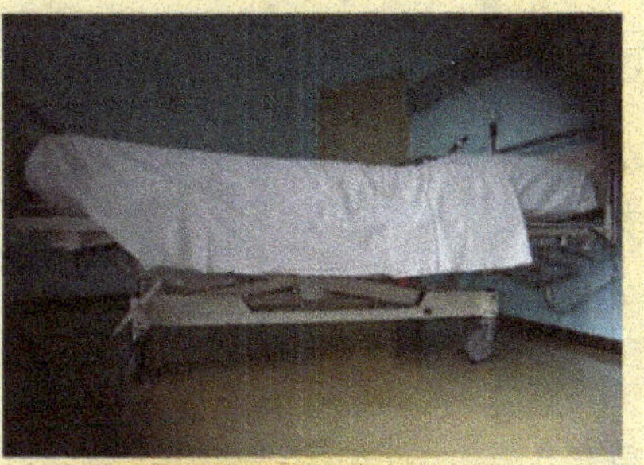 even the Marines came home. Besides, Arizona looked nothing like Vietnam. My roommate at the hospice was a nineteen-year-old punk named Morgan who slept through the chaos thanks to the methadone that the nurses tranquilized him with. I never understood why they thought it was better than the heroin he normally drilled into his arms. The kid's screams slowly gained a little bit of coherence. Under the panic and terror, he was begging someone to come rescue him. A part of me wanted to stuff my fingers in my ears. Between the junkies and the shellshock, someone always seemed to be shouting their lungs out around here. "Please," a young boy begged from the room next to mine. He was still a year or two from having puberty crack his voice. The orderlies tried to remove anything of the outside world while we were in the hospice, especially our clothes. Sleepwalking stole a lot of my modesty. Half of the city saw me walking down the highway in nothing but my skivvies and a thick coating of my own blood. It didn't feel right to race to someone's rescue in a pair of paper pajama pants. I managed to find one of Morgan's old flannel shirts. Even though it smelled of his cheep cologne, I wrapped it around my waist like a kilt. I flinched as the sleeve brushed against the fresh wounds I carved into my thighs the night before. Nurse Becky Wythe liked to think of herself as a soldier, even though her ever expanding bulk kept her from finishing boot camp. She shaved her head so close that she looked like a Marine recruit, and I had to keep from laughing every time she popped a button on her too-small nurse's uniform. When I entered the room, I saw the nurse trying to grab the boy's soiled trousers, and he kicked her square in the tits and followed up by thrusting both feet against her overhanging gut. I gave the twelve-year-old boy credit. Even though his legs were so skinny that I could make out all the bone, he managed to knock the wind out of her. "Leave me alone!" the boy demanded, tears of frustration, terror, and embarrassment running down his cheeks. The porcine woman let out a string of curses, and held her chest. She grunted, then grabbed his scrawny arms with her sausage-like fingers. He took advantage of the fact he was sweating so bad that she couldn't get a good grip. The boy bit down on her thumb and shook around like he was trying to tear off a bite-size piece. She pulled back, a small pool of blood forming on her palm. "What's wrong with you?" she yelled at him, causing him to panic even worse.

"I don't want you to see me naked!" he screamed. "I want my dad. Where's my dad? What did you do with my dad?" The kid panicked and flailed. He spat at her and prepared another donkey kick. "I don't want you to see me naked," he said over and over before sobs choked any semblance of words. "Don't be stupid," she said. "I'm a nurse. I see guys naked all the time. You don't have anything I haven't seen a thousand times before." "That doesn't change the fact that you're a woman that isn't his mother," I said, causing them both to jump. I leaned down on my haunches, making eye contact with the kid. He started wiping his eyes, so he could get a better look at me. "Get back to your room, Alvarez," Wythe said. She said something else, but I ignored her. She told me earlier in the week that she hated me and thought I was nothing but a coward. "My name is Lieutenant Mike Alvarez," I told him. "I used to be in the Army. I drove an ambulance in 'Nam and helped out at the hospitals." "Because he couldn't fight like a real man," she interjected. Wythe never resisted the urge to take a jab at me. I put my hand up and pretended like it was a wall. "Since I already had a biology degree, they ended up training me to be a nurse." The kid seemed fascinated, like most boys his age, he grew up on stories of the war. "What's your name?" "Ralphie Robinson," he said. He made a quick face. "Don't call me Ralph. I hate it when people call me Ralph." "Get out of the way and let me do my job," Wythe said, pushing me out of the way and reaching for the boy's legs again. His kick made contact with the fatty rolls on her side and she reached out to slap him. He tucked and let out a relieved breath when I caught her hand inches before it made contact with his face. "Let me take care of him," I said. "Just show me where the stuff to clean him up is. I did this all the time in 'Nam." I let it remain unspoken that I thought I could do her job ten times better than she could. She pulled away and started yelling for another nurse's aide who had a perm that went out of style twenty years ago. "I need you to help me hold him down. Get some orderlies. Tell them to bring restraints," she said. The boy curled up into a ball, staining himself from his shirt collar to his socks. "Look at me, Ralphie," I told him, trying to make myself sound as gentle as possible. "It's going to be all right." "You won't let her tie me up?" he asked hopeful. "I'm going to do what I can," I said, offering him a Boy Scout salute. "I'm not actually a nurse here, though. I'm a patient." "Got injured in the war?" I thought for a moment then nodded. "Something like that, kid." I put a hand on his shoulder and got him to relax. I thought about cleaning myself off, but I realized it would be futile until the kid himself was clean. His waste smelled sick. "Tell me about what's wrong with you? Do you have these kinds of accidents often?" When Ralphie looked ready to start crying again, I quickly added, "You don't have anything to be embarrassed of. I know you're not doing this on purpose."

"I got really bad allergies. The doctors said I would die if I stayed in Oregon, so they sent me here." He started sniffing, blue eyes widening with fear again. "I never thought my dad would just leave me here." I had to keep him talking or he would regress. "Do you have these kinds of accidents often?" I asked again. He made a disgusted face at his own smell. "I don't think you can even call them accidents. The bad plants gave me diarrhea. It hasn't stopped for over a year. Dad had to take me out of school. I can't wear…" "You have nothing to be embarrassed about. I changed diapers on bigger guys than you in the war." I forced a laugh, and he looked at me curiously. "This one Marine had a neck larger than my waist. I think I weighed less than one of his biceps." I leaned closer like I was telling a secret. "He cried a lot worse than you did whenever he needed a change. I think all those muscles softened his brain." Ralphie pictured the Marine and let out a quick giggle. Ralphie's brief moment of peace ended with him screaming. I looked behind us and saw Wythe returning with two nurses aides, the bad perm and a former Naval nurse who still called herself Ensign. They carried so many different ways to restrain the twelve-year-old boy that I was surprised one of them wasn't holding a straightjacket. "Get out of the way, Alvarez," Wythe hissed between gritted teeth. "I have things under control." Marcella Vasquez strode in with her long, unnaturally straight hair brushing behind her. She said something to me in Spanish, even though I told her repeatedly that I could barely count to five in the language. I figured out what she was saying when she held up a syringe, a smug smile on her brightly painted lips. "You promised that you wouldn't let them hurt me." Ralphie tried to climb up the wall to get away from them. Even though I figured the syringe was going to be stabbed into my arm, I stood in their way. "Just let me take care of this," I said, looking past the others and trying to force Wythe to make eye contact with me. "I think that would be an excellent idea, Mr. Alvarez." I relaxed at the sound of Sister Silencia's even tone. She raised a hand, and the nurse's aides parted out of the way. The habit made her look older than her thirty-five years, and I still tried to figure out if she was Italian, Spanish, Latino, or Portuguese. "He's not a nurse here," Wythe bit back. "He's a patient. Dr. Barghast would never allow him…" "Dr. Barghast will be back tomorrow," the nun said, taking her place beside me. "I know Mr. Alvarez's credentials. He actually has a much more outstanding resume than some of you." "He's a patient," Wythe said, trying to get into position to lunge at Ralphie again. She tried to hold her temper. Sister Silencia controlled the purse strings at the hospice. It had been dying before her sisters decided to make it their pet project and they saved it from closing. Sister Silencia looked from Ralphie to me before addressing the nurses and aides she considered 'her staff.' "Dr. Barghast's attempt to help Mr. Alvarez through his post traumatic disorder has been unsuccessful at best. I think he would be able to face some of those demons of the past if you allowed him to be useful.

Besides, the boy has made it clear to everyone in this hospital that he has no intention of letting you see him unclothed. I thought you would be thankful that someone like Mr. Alvarez is so willing to take such an unsavory responsibility away from you." "I won't allow it," Wythe said flatly. She tried to hide her smile as she crossed her arms. "I'm the head nurse, and I have the responsibility to hire and fire every nurse, aide, and clerk in this hospice." The nun smiled openly. "You seemed to have forgotten how little power you have here. I answer to the highest authority in the universe." She folded her hands and looked up to God. "I answer to the Medical Review Board," Wythe said, disgusted at the woman's religious beliefs. She motioned to her aides. "Hold him down. If Alvarez tries to get in your way, Senorita Vasquez will pump him full of lithium." "I won't stop you," Sister Silencia said, stepping out of the way. "I should inform you that I currently head the Medical Review Board. If any of you harms the boy or Mr. Alvarez, I shall have no choice but dismiss you at once." Her eyes narrowed as the aides pulled back like she'd struck them. "I can make absolutely certain that you never get hired again." "Are you threatening me?" Wythe said, the only one not intimidated by the nun. Vasquez actually left the room and went back to her desk. Sister Silencia shook her head. "I don't need to threaten you, Miss Wythe. I'm the one with all the power in this situation. If you continue to displease me, I can have this place shut down." She looked around, sniffing the air in disgust. "Sometimes I think I should shut it down anyway." "If you let me restrain the boy, you wouldn't have to worry about the smell." Ralphie cringed; everything on the bed was covered with his filth now. "I will take full responsibility for Mr. Alvarez's actions with Mr. Robinson," Sister Silencia said. "I hope that you can start taking responsibility." "Are you telling me that I don't know how to do my job?" For a moment, I thought Wythe was going to punch the nun. "You are aware that Libby Walcott hasn't stopped coughing for almost an hour now. I've tried to get an aide to help her." She turned toward the nurse's aides in the room. "I guess you were otherwise occupied." Wythe looked ready to explode. "Libby Walcott is allergic to everything. What are we supposed to do?" The tired smile on the nun's face told me that she was tired of discussing things. "These children require a very septic room. You need to scrub down their rooms at least once a day, preferably with alcohol." She walked over to the wall, and ripped off some peeling paint. "This place is crawling with mold and dry rot. I can't believe you brought a boy with that delicate of a constitution to stay in this room." Wythe started to say something but the cry of shock that left the nun's throat cut her off. "Are these mushrooms?" She pulled some sienna and purple fungus out of the wall. "Mushrooms are not very allergenic," Wythe said. She tried to sound confident, but I could tell she was suddenly very nervous. "Mr. Robinson is not spending the night here," Sister Silencia said, letting us know that there would be no more argument. "

"Take him to your room once he is cleaned up, Mr. Alvarez. I shall arrange for a rollaway bed." "You can bet I plan on telling Dr. Barghast about this tomorrow," Wythe said, stomping out as quickly as her waddle would allow. The aides looked at each other nervously before they followed. Sister Silencia handed me some supplies and gave me a very serious look. "That boy is your responsibility now, Mr. Alvarez. Keep him safe." Morgan slipped out of his restraints and stole every blanket in the room. He rocked back and forth on his bunk, sweating and shivering at the same time. Snot slid into his mouth when he tried to smile. "Don't do drugs," he told Ralphie, blinking away the perspiration that stung his eyes. "This is Ralphie," I explained. "He's going to be staying with us. His room has some kind of mushroom infestation." "Whole place is falling apart," Morgan said, his teeth chattering loudly. I noticed his hands were covered in dried blood from scratching at the scabs on his arms. "Are you all right?" Ralphie asked. "Do you have bad allergies, too?" Instead of answering the kid, Morgan covered his hands with the blankets. "I'm worried about that girl down the hall," he said when the silence started to become too uncomfortable. "It sounds like she's going to cough out a lung." "Sister Silencia told Wythe to clean up her room and check on her," I told him. "I guess there really wasn't anything they could do for her." Morgan hated Wythe almost as much as I did. When his parents dropped him off, she smashed all of his vinyl records and set his magazines on fire. "Bitch never showed up. I've been watching for nurses all night. I think they're letting that poor girl choke herself to death." Ralphie stared at me. "Can't you help her, Alvarez?" "I'll see what I can do." I swallowed as I took my first steps toward Libby Walcott's room, terrified it was already too late. Morgan and Ralphie followed me, as scared as they were hopeful. Libby Walcott cried each time she coughed up more blood. Her face was covered in a mask of mucus and saliva. Every time she tried to talk, her throat seized up and refused to let her. She tried to sit up, only to choke even more. "Is that going to happen to me?" Ralphie whispered. He stared at her. "She's not going to die, is she? You know something that can make her feel all better, right? I saw a guy stop a woman from choking to death in a movie. You know how to do stuff like that, right?" I didn't answer. Libby Walcott looked no more than seven or eight; her brown hair was matted and filthy. Her hand shook as she reached out, and I took it gently. "You're not alone anymore," I said. I expected Sister Silencia to storm in like she always did, yelling at the nurse's aides and probably a doctor or two, but the nun never appeared. "Has someone come to check on you?" I asked. "They took Emily away," she managed to wheeze out as she weakly pointed to the bed beside her, the white sheets stained brown from old blood. "They zipped her up and took her away in a bag." "Did...she...die?" Ralphie asked, trying his hardest not to cry in front of a girl. I felt him next to me, so I put a comforting arm around him and hoped Libby wouldn't answer the question. "There was a lady in white," Libby started.

Anything else she wanted to say was stolen from her by heavy wheezing. I watched her eyes roll back in her head, as she started lurching. "Get a doctor!" I yelled at Morgan. "Get a nurse, anything." He gave me a nod and ran out, leaving a trail of sweat-stained blankets behind him. "What's happening to her?" Ralphie asked. "Anaphylaxis," I said. "I've seen people react this way to medication. Some foods can cause people with severe allergies to do this." The little girl's convulsions grew worse, and the seizure threw her off the bed. "I've never seen this happen from just the air." Ralphie tensed beside me. At first, I thought he was just scared. He grabbed his stomach, and his face twisted in pain. The smell of infection and diarrhea filled the room. "I need you to get out of here," I told him. "It's not safe for you." He tried to walk, but the pain doubled him over. "Can you walk?" "No," he whimpered. I looked from one kid to the other, trying to figure out what I should do. I doubted that Libby Walcott could even see me, might have even forgotten I was there. In the war, we learned that saving one was better than killing two. I picked up the cringing form of Ralphie Robinson and prepared to leave. I normally hated to hear Marcella Vasquez chorus of rapid fire Spanish and the fact she was convinced my name was really Miguel and not Mike, but I wanted to kiss her when I heard her storm in. She pushed us out of the way, and I stumbled to the floor, trying to cushion Ralphie's landing. That was when I saw the jungle of mushrooms growing under Libby Walcott's bed. I never saw so much fungus. I knew it couldn't have just been neglect. They grew out of the bottom of the mattress and the springs. I saw the spores floating in the air. "Get her off the bed. Get her out of the bedroom!" Vasquez glared at me. "Your boy smells terrible. Get him out of here!" Wythe came in with her usual suspects. "What are they doing out of their room? Vasquez, get these patients back to their room now." She glared at me. "I thought you were going to clean him up." I reached under the bed and pulled out a mushroom. "What is this stuff?" I asked. "It's making her sick." Wythe slapped it out of my hand. "Get back to your room right now," she said. I never saw her look so scared. I knew I'd caught her doing something. "If you're not gone in ten seconds, I swear I'll make sure you never see this kid again." I stared at the mushroom in my hand. "We need to go, Ralphie." I picked the boy up, holding my breath at the smell of him. I wondered how many accidents he'd had since he was exposed to the fungus. "This is important," I said, pushing the mushroom into Vasquez's hand. She barely heard me, just continued to babble in Spanish as she worked. The mushroom fell to the floor, and Wythe quickly crushed it under her heel. Even though my family stopped speaking Spanish around the time of the Gadsden Purchase, I managed to make out three words that Vasquez kept repeating: 'five, children' and 'dead.' The former Mrs. Barghast happily destroyed her husband's military career when she showed up at their divorce proceedings armed with pictures of him with various teenage girls. The judge awarded the house, car, and most of Dr. Barghast's income to the wife when she recognized his fifteen-year-old niece in one of the more explicit pictures.

The doctor never learned anything. If anyone had listened to the various junkie girls that got dropped off at the hospice by their parents, they would have arrested him for molestation. "I wanted to thank you for helping out last night, Mike," Wythe said, bringing over a chair and sitting down. She raised an eyebrow and the psychiatrist nodded at her. "I was out of line, and I appreciate you helping us with that boy, Ralph Robinson." She smiled, and I prepared for the hammer to drop. "But you had no business sneaking into that girl's room last night." A couple of the junkies hooted and cheered. "Libby Walcott almost died because of the two of you," Wythe continued. "You got in the way while we were trying to save her life." "Libby's all right?" Ralphie chimed in. "Can I go see her?" Dr. Barghast never broke eye contact but he motioned to Ralphie. "Make him leave. He doesn't belong here. This is meant for the mental patients, not those suffering from allergies." "I'll take him back to my room," I said, starting to stand. "He's a big boy, Mr. Alvarez," Dr. Barghast said. "I'm sure that he can make his way back on his own. Besides, I doubt you want him to hear what I have to say to you." Ralphie gave me a frightened look, so I lied to him and told him that everything would be fine. "What's going on?" I asked, when I was certain Ralphie was out of earshot. Morgan looked at me and shrugged. "You had an episode last night," Wythe said. "It nearly cost that little girl her life. You were ranting about some poison mushrooms killing her. She was having a very simple coughing fit, but you mistook it for an extreme allergic reaction caused by some kind of demon mushrooms." I took a deep breath to keep my temper. "Sister Silencia saw mushrooms in Ralphie's room and then I found them in Libby Walcott's room. The bottom of her bed was covered in them. I showed you one of those mushrooms." Wythe shook her head, and I wondered when she became such a good actress. "No, you didn't have anything in your hand." "He wasn't freaking out," Morgan said. "I was there." "Did you see the mushrooms?" Dr. Barghast asked. "I suppose you could have seen all kinds of mushrooms. You see all kinds of things these days." A couple of the 'shell shocks' laughed at him. Morgan shifted uncomfortably. "He wasn't freaking out, Doc. Vasquez was so panicked that she kept forgetting to speak English." "She told me that five children died here lately," I said. "Libby said they took her roommate out in a body bag." "Do you know anything about people that have frequent allergy attacks, Mr. Alvarez?" Dr. Barghast asked, a smug smile curling at the corner of his lips. "They start to get a feeling of panic and imagine their own demise and that of others. You listened to the delusions of a very sick girl and she triggered your flashbacks." "Where is Libby Walcott?" I asked. Wythe looked like I punched her in the gut. She never planned on me asking such a simple question. "We had to move her to a hospital," she said so quickly I was surprised when everyone didn't get suspicious. "She'll be back when she recovers." "Look in her room," I said. "You'll find those mushrooms under her bed." I turned toward Wythe. "Your nurses had to see them."

Dr. Barghast shook his head and let out a sigh. "I think it would be helpful for you if you told us about the events that led to your discharge from the Army." "What?" I said. "Why?" The psychiatrist leaned closer, and Wythe stifled a laugh. "Start with telling us what you did during the war." I took a deep breath, blocking out the sounds of screams in my head. "The military offered me a non-combat position as an ambulance driver, because they considered me too fragile for the front. I had a degree in biology, and I figured that patching up troops was the next best thing to teaching high school science." "Coward," Wythe whispered under her breath. "I volunteered for extra duty. I helped out in the hospital. When they needed someone to help at the morgue, I figured it couldn't be too bad. I saw many kids come in that couldn't be saved, though, some with body parts missing. Some were no older than seventeen." Morgan looked at me. "You never told me you worked in the morgue. What was it like with all those bodies?" "One of the bags moved," I said, my eyes narrowing. "I heard this kid screaming. They had zipped a living boy inside a body bag, then piled other dead bodies on top of him. By the time I found him, a young Marine named Watersford, he died of asphyxiation." "You knew him?" Dr. Barghast asked, already knowing the answer. "His name was Shane Watersford, just some freckled Marine kid from South Carolina. He hated hippies, but he had a crush on Grace Slick. He used to sing her songs while in the shower stalls, horribly off key." I shrugged. "We talked about movies we liked, and he would read the gory parts of dime store sci-fi to me when I was taking care of him. You made friends pretty quickly there." "How did he end up in the morgue?" Dr. Barghast probed. "A bullet shattered most of his left hand. It was the kind of injury that left a boy with a hook, not a toe tag. I knew it couldn't have just been a simple mistake. I decided to do a little exploring." I let out a sigh, the memories so strong I could smell the lye and formaldehyde. "I found three other boys that had been tortured to death and not by the Viet Cong—all red heads." "A serial killer in the middle of a war?" Morgan said, shocked. "Isn't that a bit redundant?" "That must have been horrible for you," Dr. Barghast said. "No wonder you got shell shocked." I swallowed my fear, reminding myself that Arizona was not Vietnam. "Worst thing to happen to me since boot camp." Wythe laughed. "I should've known you would have a problem finishing boot camp." I thought back to the screams being bludgeoned out of Koichi's throat, Sergeant Conroy's gory salute, and the explosion in the barracks. "My boot camp was exceptionally difficult," I said. "That's why the Army thought I was too fragile for the infantry." I smiled nervously. "They were right." "Tell us what happened next," Dr. Barghast said. "I started sleepwalking, which I guess was the start of my mental problems," I admitted. "Things got worse when I decided to help the military police catch him. The coroner, James Anthony Newell, killed a bunch of people in Texas. We knew it was him, and I helped catch him. He cut me up a lot, but we caught him. If I hadn't started cutting myself in my sleep, the military police said I would have gotten a medal."

Dr. Barghast nodded like it all made sense. "I hope you all understand what you've heard." "Yeah," Morgan said, offering me a sympathetic hand. "War really is Hell." Mr. Alvarez suffered from severe flashbacks when he thought the little girl was dying. He created a conspiracy in his mind. Whenever someone gets sick, he believes it's the result of a psychotic killer." He turned to me. "It was just a sick little girl. She's all right. There's no killer and no killer mushrooms." "I didn't imagine it," I said, standing up suddenly. Dr. Barghast remained calm. "I think you need to really think about what happened to you. We all appreciate everything you've done for us and our country, but you've got to remember that this isn't Vietnam." I wanted to scream about how I did that every morning, but I knew it wouldn't help my case. "Vasquez told me five children have already died," I argued. "How do you explain that?" Wythe raised an eyebrow. "I thought you didn't speak Spanish. How do you know what she said?" "We all see things," one of the other shell shocks said. "It's nothing to be embarrassed about. My wife was cutting up carrots and I slapped her in the face before I realized my hand had moved. I thought she was a Cong with a machete." A former pilot nodded in agreement. "Every time I hear a car backfire, I swear it feels like I'm flying." He shook his head at his own misery. "I'm afraid what's going to happen next Fourth of July." He let out a deep sigh, then flinched at an imagined enemy. "I hate all those fireworks." Dr. Barghast folded his hands. "I hate to embarrass you, Mr. Alvarez," he said, giving Wythe a knowing look, "but I think you need to realize that your judgment can sometimes be… compromised." A heavily-tattooed former Ranger who cried himself to sleep every night said, "We're gonna be here for you, buddy." "I think it would be best for everyone if you stayed away from the allergy ward," Dr. Barghast said. He waited to get some acknowledgement from a couple others in the group. Wythe pretended to yawn to hide her grin. "We appreciate your help with the Robinson boy. You can continue to take care of him, unless we think you might become a danger to him." "If I catch you trying to sneak back into the allergy ward," Wythe said happily, "I'll make sure you never see the kid again." "Do you understand me?" Dr. Barghast asked, speaking to me like I was a child. I could hear the pride underneath his voice. He knew he'd won. I bit my lower lip. "Do you understand?" he repeated the words again, slower, letting me know how serious he was. I understood everything he was trying to say: If you don't obey us, we'll kill your little friend, Ralphie. My brain showed me a slide show filled with various people I knew had died. I didn't think my sanity could handle adding Ralphie to the list. I imagined his face swollen up as his waste turned bloodier and bloodier. Morgan slammed a fist on the arm of his chair. "Mike wasn't freaking out or anything. I believe him." "Let me ask you a question, Mr. Alvarez… Mike," Dr. Barghast said, and I realized what it felt like to be caught in a spiderweb. "Do you think that myself and the staff are actually trying to murder these children?" "Of course not, Doctor," I lied. When Morgan and I returned to our room, Ralphie was crying and clutching a piece of paper while holding his stomach.

When I tried to approach him, he pushed me away and ran into the closet, shutting the door behind him. Morgan started to say something, but I put a finger to my lips. He made a motion like he was zipping his lips shut and plopped down on his bed. I knocked on the closet door. "Ralphie, I told you that you don't have to be embarrassed. I'll clean you up." "I know," Ralphie replied, his voice heavy with the weight of depression. "I don't care about that." "Well we do," Morgan said. "Let him clean you up before I pass out from the smell." Ralphie opened the closet a crack and handed me the piece of paper. I took a few moments to look it over and said, "I'm sorry." I tried to think of something else to say, but I just ended up apologizing a second time. A part of me wanted to lie to him, but I knew that would make it worse. "What's wrong?" Morgan asked. "Ralphie's dad won't be coming back for him," I said. "He thinks his dad's left him here to die." I went back to the clipboard and discovered the oldest motive in the book: Dr. Barghast was cashing checks sent by parents convinced that there children were still alive, only not getting better. "You're not dying," Morgan said, looking at me to verify that. "Where did you get this, Ralphie?" I asked, coaxing him out. He made sure the door was closed and whispered, "I sneaked into that girl's room." Ralphie thought a moment. "I think they set her bed on fire, the one you said was covered in all those mushrooms." "I knew you didn't hallucinate that," Morgan said triumphantly. I let out a long sigh. "I need you to get Ralphie out of here tonight, Morgan. I was lying when I said they weren't killing kids. Barghast, Wythe, and who knows who else really are killing kids around here." I grabbed some cleaning supplies and Ralphie went to the bed so I could wash him. "You're getting rid of me, too." Ralphie almost jumped up in the middle of me cleaning him up, but I put a comforting hand on his chest. "You and Morgan are gonna wait at my apartment until I leave this place, too," I said. "If I can get Sister Silencia's help, I'm sure she'll get one of the other Sisters to get me out of here." "They're trying to kill me?" Ralphie asked, and I gently covered his mouth. "I won't let them," I assured him. "I'm going to do my best to keep from hurting you anymore." I looked at him. "Don't go back to the allergy wing for any reason, Ralphie. That place is poison. The reason you had an allergy attack is that your room is covered with mushrooms." "Okay," he said, "How much danger are we in?" Morgan asked. He looked more scared that the little kid. "You can use a knife to defend yourself, right?" I asked. "If anyone but me shows up at the door, grab a knife from the nurse's kitchen." "I don't think I can do that," Morgan said. I made him look me in the eye. "If anyone comes for you, it means that I'm dead. They killed me. You two will be next if you don't take one of the kitchen knives, shove it into their gut nice and deep, then twist." Morgan nodded. "I thought you didn't like violence." "I don't," I said. "But you won't believe what I've had to do to survive and protect those that I love."

October 31, 1976
Morgan convinced one of his friends to bring him a Batman Halloween costume. For a moment, Ralphie got lost in the act of dressing up and trick-or-treating for the first time in his life.

When he noticed me keeping watch, his enthusiasm dropped. "Maybe you should go with us," he said. His face lit up with hope. "The three of us could keep running until we reached Mexico. They wouldn't chase us there." "If I did," I said, handing him the plastic mask, "then I'd feel responsible for all the kids they killed after we left." Morgan slid on his swimming suit and a pair of kitchen gloves to complete his makeshift Robin costume. He shoved a pipe into his Halloween sack. "We'll take the long way back to your house, and get lost in the trick-or-treating kids out on the street." He parted his hair to the side and cut off the spikes. He looked like he was fourteen or fifteen in that get up. Ralphie looked at me nervously. "Don't get worried if you get to your house and we're not there yet. We'll probably still be out getting candy." "I'm going to wait a few hours after you leave before I sneak into the allergy ward." They exchanged frightened glances. "I've met enough Rangers and Marines to teach me some basic stealth. I won't have a problem getting in." "Are you sure we can't stay and help?" Ralph asked hopefully. "We're already dressed for crime fighting." He let out a quick laugh and elbowed Morgan playfully in the ribs. "You two are helping me by escaping," I told them. Morgan picked the lock to the window and took out a makeshift rope he'd made from a pair of sheets. "Just like the Caped Crusaders," he joked. He packed up some more supplies and tried to act brave. "Are you sure you don't want to come with us? They're the killers, not you. We can call the cops. Maybe they'll find something." I shook my head. "No, I have to do this myself." Ralphie hugged me tightly, and Morgan looked like he wanted to do the same. "I don't like saying goodbye," he said, wiping his nose on the sleeve of his costume. "Have fun trick-or-treating," I said. "Save me some candy, okay?" "Sure, man, and we'll stay up all night and watch the scary movie marathon," Morgan said. By the time I checked the door again, the two of them were gone and I could finally let out the worried breath I was holding. A nun named Sister Corazon breezed in shortly after nightfall, wearing cat ears and felt tail outside of her habit for a costume. "Excuse me," she said to a red-headed receptionist who smelled of pot, "I'm looking for Sister Silencia. We haven't seen her all day. She never came home. She was supposed to take the kids trick-or-treating." Her smile never faded, even though her eyebrows furled with fear. "I don't know," the receptionist said, angry that the nun was killing her buzz. "You nuns all look the same." "She's not here," I told the nun as I walked up behind her, remembering how Libby Walcott had tried to tell me something about Sister Silencia before her illness got the better of her. "My name's Mike Alvarez. The Sister and I used to talk about working in hospitals during the war. I hope she's all right." We walked away from the receptionist who was glad to be rid of us. Sister Corazon laughed. "Oh, I'm sure she's fine. If a coyote or a bear attacked her, she'd probably bite them first." She spoke low, her brown eyes looking around. "Please tell me if you find her." She tried to say something to me in Spanish but I shook my head, regretting for the first time in my life that I never learned the language. "She thought something funny was going on here," she said in a low voice.

"Look, it's important that I check on someone," I said, wondering if it was wrong to put my trust in this woman. "Can you make a distraction for me? Make a big deal about needing to see Sister Silencia, that'll work?" The nun giggled. "Okay, sure, I can do that for you." She blushed slightly and I think she liked me, despite her being a nun. "This is like being in a James Bond film." She forced herself to frown and walked back over to the receptionist, now looking distraught. It wasn't long until several nurses and aides wandered over to try to calm her down. I didn't see Wythe amongst them and I snuck away. They had locked the door to the room, but Morgan wasn't the only one who knew how to pick a lock. As I entered, I scrunched my nose. The place smelled of feces, blood, vomit, and rot. Under the usual filth of sickness, I recognized the smell of a dead body. A little boy sneezing blood reached up to me. They had bound him to the iron bed frame. He looked around six, and he freaked me out beyond the ability to describe in words. Each sneeze was followed by a howl of pain. The entire lower half of his face was a mask of dried blood, and flies buzzed around him. "It's all right," I said, "I'll get you out of this." "What's going on?" he asked, speaking as quickly as possible before another sneezing fit hit him. I checked under his bed for mushrooms, and I discovered small amounts of the fungus starting to grow out of some kind of meat they had coated the base of the bed with. Their killer mushrooms were some kind of parasite. I reached underneath and probed the meat until something small dropped on my arm. The little boy screamed, and I wanted to join in when I realized it was a human eye. "Oh my God, they're using the victims to feed this thing," I said, lurching up a good deal of my dinner. The kid started to ask questions, but I got his bonds loose and pushed him out the door. "Don't stop running until you find a nun. Her name's Sister Corazon. She'll get you to safety." He looked at me confused. "Run!" I yelled. I showed him the human eye to show him how much danger he was in. He clumsily made his way out of the ward, stumbling more than running. I found the body of a little girl lying on a mattress covered with the mushrooms in the far corner. I bent down to check if she was alive, when I realized that the fungus was growing out of her. I closed the little girl's eyes, wondering if the body was Libby Walcott's old roommate, Emily, or just another nameless victim. They had left the basement door open, and I knew it was a trap. I also knew the answers I was looking were waiting for me down there. I screamed when I saw Sister Silencia lying at the base of the stairs with her throat slashed. Her blood had congealed around her, feeding both the flies and the fungus. I put my hand on the wall and I pulled it back when I felt it squish. Dr. Barghast and Wythe had turned the entire basement into a breeding ground! "I know what you're thinking," Dr. Barghast said from out of the darkness. "But I'm not technically a killer." He walked up, ankle deep in his poison fungus. "We exposed the children to the mushrooms, but it was their illness that actually killed them. As you can tell, someone without their allergies has no ill effects from them. They died of their allergies." He put his hand over his heart. "It happens all the time, sadly." "Uh-huh, and did a mushroom stab Sister Silencia?" I asked.

Dr. Barghast feigned disgust. "That wasn't my fault, either. I told Wythe to stop her. I never said anything about killing her. She took my orders a little too far. I thought she would just tie her up down here. " "For how long? Until you killed a thousand children?" "I told you I'm not a killer!" he ranted before quickly regaining his composure. "These children were going to die anyway. We just saved them from suffering any longer. They die a little bit quicker, and we get the money to keep this place going. If I figured this out years ago, I never would've begged that nun for the money to save the hospice." "It's over," I said. "I freed one of your kids. He'll find help and talk to the cops about what you've been doing to him and the others." I didn't realize he was distracting me until a second before I felt a machete split the air behind me. I ducked just in time to receive a harsh scratch on my back, and I kicked the weapon out of Wythe's hand. I followed it up with a right jab to the jaw, and the nurse fell back, shocked. "We'll blame you for Sister Silencia's murder," Wythe gasped as she recovered from my blow. "You're the mental patient. We'll just tell them you started shouting in Vietnamese. You have a terrible reputation around here already. People expect Vietnam veterans to go crazy and start killing people, even a coward like you." "You forgot one thing," I said. The two of them waited for me to answer. "Sister Silencia was smarter than all of us. She told people that she knew you were up to something. There's a nun upstairs right now investigating her disappearance. That nun believes you're responsible already." Dr. Barghast paced back and forth, his own madness and paranoia becoming more obvious. "This is all your fault, you stupid bitch," he yelled at Wythe. "You killed a fucking nun! They'll fry your fat ass!" "What are you talking about, Doctor?" Wythe asked, worried and confused. "You wouldn't let anything happen to me, would you?" I saw the look in her eyes, the way she looked at the doctor, and realized there was something between them. My stomach turned at the idea of the two of them being lovers. She started to run to him, but he slapped her across the face and turned to leave. "Where are you going?" she asked, her face red from where he struck her. When he didn't answer the question, she started to scream the question. I heard people running into the room above us. "Getting the hell out of here before the cops come to arrest you!" he yelled at her. "I'll try to stall them for as long as possible." "But I can't leave without you," Wythe cried "I love you!" She looked like she was falling apart and I wondered what she would do next. Dr. Barghast started to say something snide to her, but the knife she stuck deep in his throat stopped him cold. She twisted the blade around. She sawed at his throat, but couldn't slice through his spinal cord. He kept screaming and gurgling long after he was actually dead as she yelled, "I love you! I can't live without you! If we can't be together then there's no point!" As the doctor lay dead on the floor, she stood still, then slowly she turned to face me, the blood dripping from the tip of the knife. "This is your fault," she hissed. "Everything was perfect until you stuck your nose into things." She let out a primal howl. "I wanted a happy life! I wanted a knight in shining armor!

You destroyed everything!" She searched her brain for the worst word she could think of to hurt me and came up with. "You coward." A thousand memories of war and death floated through my head, and I gave her the same smile I once gave a psychopathic coroner once. "I have a secret," I said in a low voice, even using the same words. "I actually have killed someone before. We kill to survive, you see. Humans are just animals." The nurse lunged at me with her knife, and I twisted out of the way and slammed an open palm into her side. She let out an angry grunt, and I grabbed her arm and contorted it to the point just before it broke; the knife fell to the floor. Wythe spat curses at me, threatening me with torture and death. I shook my head and calmly picked up some of the mushrooms. "I'm not allergic," she said. "Do you know how many times I've…" Terror froze the words in her mouth when she saw the look in my eye, one of no mercy, and she started to beg for her life. "I don't know anything about these plants," I said. "I don't know if force feeding them to you is going to kill you or not, but I know I'm sure gonna try." I shoved one of them into her mouth and squeezed the juices down her throat as she began to choke. "I'm not a killer," I said softly. "Maybe you'll survive this, but then again, maybe you won't." She tried to vomit up the poisons, but I forced down the bile with more mushrooms. Her body started jerking, and she choked on her tongue before the poison had fully worked its way into her system. I knew I'd killed her, regardless of how she actually died. I vowed never to delude myself and end up like her or the doctor. I walked out of the basement without looking back as people rushed by me and down the stairs. By the time anyone figured out what had happened, I would be long gone. Morgan and Ralphie were waiting for me at home, and I knew the cops would show up to ask a thousand questions before the night was through. But I already knew the answers and what I would tell them if they tried to pin the deaths on me. "I have shell shock, Officers. I blacked out when I realized Nurse Wythe had killed the nun. I don't know what happened after that." After all, I'd used that excuse before and it had worked then, too.

Shawn Conn

LDP: What type of mediums do you work with?

SC: Like a lot of artists from my generation, we all started out using traditional mediums and have gradually introduced, or switched over to digital art. I paint with acrylic, use graphite and colored pencil and work digitally, sometimes combining both traditional and digital mediums.

LDP: What inspired you to be an artist?

SC: Art runs in my family on my mother's side and I've been creating art ever since I was old enough to hold a pencil. From a very young age I knew I was going to be an artist and my parents definitely encouraged it in me. Our house was always filled with comic books, and it was always Godzilla movies on Saturday afternoons. Then we'd stay up late with my dad watching Gregory the Gravewalker and the Hammer films and classic monster movies.

LDP: Do you feel people are born with artistic talent, or that it's something to be learned?

SC: I believe everyone is born with artistic talent. It's parental and/or societal influence that then plays an important part in whether we continue to create art and grow as artists, or give into the practicality of the 9 to 5 world. Personally, I'm glad it's a small club. Those utopian art societies always end badly.

LDP: What do you think is the biggest change from Old-World art to Modern day art?

SC: I think the most obvious change is the introduction of the digital medium. It's becoming more and more of a prominent medium in the art world at large. It's been a mainstay of the entertainment, graphic design and illustration industries for quite some time now and it's now being introduced to the fine art world.
The fine art world is traditionally always resistant to change, or new things, but once it becomes such a force, I don't think the fine art world will have much of a choice. The problem with digital art in the fine art realm though, will be the very thing that makes it so desirable with the aforementioned industries. That's the ease at which it can be reproduced. Although a traditionally created artwork can be reproduced, and often is, there will still only ever be one original. Digital art will never be able to make that claim.

LDP: What do you think traditional/classic art can teach about horror in history?

SC: Classic art is rife with horror, both real and imagined. From the earliest cave paintings depicting the terrifying beasts of early man's time to the bizarre creatures and gods represented in the art of the early Americas, then onto the depictions of Hell by artists like Hieronymus Bosch during the Renaissance all the way to the modern era and the horrific art of artists like Francis Bacon. Or the bizarre fantasy worlds of Odilon Redon, Salvador Dali, etc. Even more, today's Pop Surrealists depict horror in a sickly sweet way that leaves the viewer feeling slightly uneasy. As long as there are horrors in the world and man continues to brutalize man, artists will always try to make sense of it, satirize it, condemn it, or just to simply depict it.

LDP: Do you ever use symbolism in your art?

SC: I'm not sure one can ever get away from using symbolism in his or her art. Art, by its very nature is a symbolic gesture. Every time I create art, whether it is fine art or an illustration, I'm keenly aware of the impetus for the artwork and keep it firmly in mind as I progress through the piece. If I start to deviate from my intended message, I'll readjust the art, start over or even walk away to get a fresh perspective.

LDP: Can you think of a popular piece of art that really should be categorized as horror art?

SC: Anything that Thomas Kinkade paints. Nothing that serene can be all hunky dory. The gingerbread house in Hansel & Gretel, Camp Crystal Lake, Elm St. All come to mind.

LDP: Does horror writing help you draw?

SC: Most definitely. If I'm illustrating a cover for a horror novel, or anthology magazine then, if at all possible, I try to read excerpts from the story (ies). Even better, I try to have either the author or editor pick out one or two passages that they feel best sum up the whole novel or anthology. The same goes for when I'm creating a self-promotional illustration

or a fine art piece. If it's my own horrific creation, I'll create the story in my head as I'm working through the initial sketches, all the way to the final stroke. Sometimes, I'll even write down the story to get a better visual of where I want to end up. It's also a good way of supplying subject matter for future work.

SC: I think it can be a valuable tool to the artist, if done with the right intentions and if done constructively. The unfortunate truth, however, is that with the advent of the blog and forum, anyone with an internet connection can become an instant critic. All too often someone with an axe to grind or someone who is just plain mean, takes it upon themselves to educate the masses as to what's wrong with a particular artist's work, or even entire art movements. I was part of an art forum once, where a particularly nasty "critic" derided everyone's work, even a 12 year old girl. Anytime someone offers a critique, whether it be of a technical nature, or an esoteric one, it should be done to elevate the artist, or art to a higher place. Not to make a self-important, pompous asshole's day because he crushed someone's ego.

I don't listen to what art critics say. I don't know anybody who needs a critic to find out what art is.
-Jean Michel Basquiat

SC: I blame my parents. Every Saturday afternoon at 1 p.m. there would be a monster movie on, usually a Godzilla film, or one of the classic monster movies. My brother Mike and I would be right there glued to the TV.

Then Saturday nights, after the 11 o' clock news, and that famous tagline, "It's 11:30. Do you know where your children are?" We would stay up with my dad to watch Gregory the Gravewalker's show and he usually featured Hammer films, followed up by a cult classic, like "Trog" or "The Frozen Dead." In the summer, my parents would take us to the drive in to see movies like "The Food of the Gods," "Willard," "The Incredible Melting Man" and on and on. By the time I reached junior high, I was already deeply entrenched in the horror, sci-fi and fantasy genres and it showed in my evolving art ability. That was about the time my mom introduced me to the horror novel and sealed the deal. I always think it's kind of ironic that I associate horror with feelings of contentment and happiness.

SC: Very much so. Whether it is the science behind Dr. Frankenstein's experiments, the biology behind giant and mutated creatures, or the straight up sci-fi horror of movies like "Alien," sci-fi and horror will always be intertwined. Science, even if stretched to the limits of plausibility, gives validation to the horrific. I actually have a series of paintings planned for the near future centered on sci-fi horror.

SC: I'd have to say, my favorite horror film to date is "Dawn of the Dead '04," but its predecessor, the Romero "Dawn of the Dead," completely changed the course of my art career. I was into sci-fi, fantasy & horror my whole life and I actually thought about going on for a career in special FX. Then, one dark night, up late and watching TV in my room, a trailer for this movie unlike anything I had ever seen came on. It was all of these bluish green, undead people shambling around a mall and they were eating the living! At the very end of the trailer they showed the scene of the zombies bursting through the elevator doors. It terrified me. I became obsessed with drawing zombies and scenes of a zombie apocalypse.

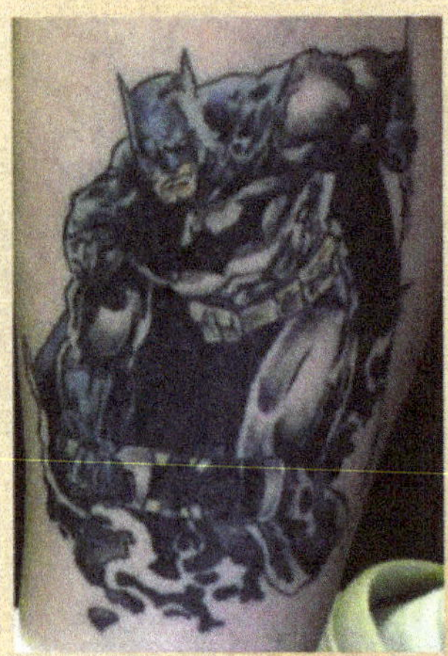

The more I drew and painted them, the more I became aware of the dark side of my own psyche and horror became the impetus for the direction I wanted to go with my art.

LDP: Do you aim for a specific audience, or do you feel your art may appeal to the general public?

SC: I think, to a certain degree that most horror, fantasy & sci-fi artists create art with a specific target in mind, whether it's a conscious or sub-conscious effort. Every painting tells a story and to that end, it's aimed at a specific genre, which in turn attracts a specific audience. However, I have to imagine that a lot of artists, like me, create art that you hope will elevate you to the status of a Frazetta, Gogos, or Vallejo and the same time of mass public appeal that they commanded. I know I have this secret fantasy to see my work on the sides of pimped-out vans. Doesn't everyone?

LDP: Do you think digital art is as valid an art form as traditional mediums?

SC: That kind of depends on the arena. As far as fine art goes, its gaining ground, thanks largely to the pop surrealist and lowbrow art movements, but it has a way to go before it will be recognized by the more conservative fine art community. It's looked at as the realm of the graphic designer and illustrator, which is where it's gained the most respect as an extremely useful and ever evolving tool. Digital art has enabled illustrators and designers the ability to complete projects in a relatively short period of time, which means more time to produce and happy art directors.

I also know of a large number of artists, myself included, who create work using both traditional and digital art forms and more often than not combine the two. As far as quality goes, I think digital art has really opened the door to push the limits of what defines art and who it belongs to. Just about anyone who can use a mouse, or pen tool and has the right software can create art now. I think it's good in that it's helped open doors for talented artists, who otherwise wouldn't have the ability to go to art school. The downside is just about anyone who can use a mouse, or pen tool and has the right software can create art now, and that can make it tough for potential clients to weed through the mass amounts of mediocre, or downright awful art. If an artist is going to get the job, then he has to figure out creative ways to attract the attention of potential clients, right from the get go. Then, have the art to back it up.

LDP: Animation viewed as art in motion is a great phenomenon; would you like to be an animator? And if so, what kind of animation would you produce?

SC: Throughout my entire career as an artist, I've wanted to explore every possible medium I can. Animation is no different. My oldest daughter is in school right now for CGI animation and it rekindled that old desire to explore it as a creative outlet. I've always wanted to do an animation based on my art and breathing life into some of my static creatures. I have a pretty busy schedule these days, but at some point I'll start delving into it more.

LDP: Can you think of an incident of real horror that might have compelled you to produce horror art?

SC: Trigonometry. There's nothing more horrific to an artist than higher math. I've seen some gruesome thing and have definitely experienced some scary moments i my life and I'm sure they've helped to shape me both as a person and as an artist. But to say there was a definin moment that singularly pushed me into horror art, didn really happen...that I know of. I will say this. At around 12, maybe 13, I saw the movie Helter Skelter, and then read the book by Vincent Bugliosi and Curt Gentry detailing the horrific crimes committed by Charles Manson and his "family." It was my first real glimpse int the truly dark and evil acts that man is capable of. That story scared the hell out of me and stayed with me for a long time.

LDP: Like Vampires and Werewolves before them, the Zombie genre is changing in current form, what type of Zombies do you feel are scarier, running ghouls or walking ones?

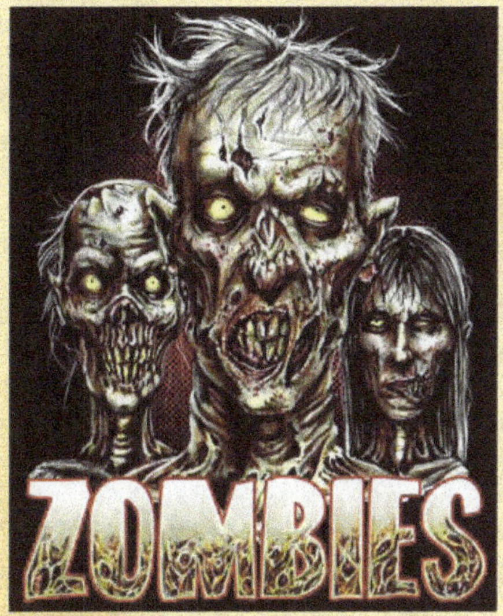

SC: Well, when I was younger I would've said, "Who cares!? Bring the nasty, flesh-eatin' beasties on!" Now that I'm a bit older, I'm definitely opting for the slow ones. The fast ones are definitely much scarier, as evidenced by films like "Dawn of the Dead '04" and "28 Days/Weeks Later." The whole concept of an undead person, who you may, or may not know, wanting to eat you and at the same time infect you is scary enough. Add the ability to outrun you and you've got a full blown "Holy shit!" scenario. It's kind of why I started getting in shape again.

LDP: Do you feel there is a credible difference in sensual art and pornographic art?

SC: Without a doubt. I think sensual is a lot harder to pull off as an art form, than pornographic. No pun intended. Pornography, whether it's soft core, hardcore, or just MTV, reality TV, or shows like "Desperate Housewives," etc., has inundated our lives and our children's lives. Even shows on networks like the Disney Channel have their fair share of innuendos. As a father, I think it's gone too far into our daily lives and our children's lives for sure. It's become the "sure sell" for marketing execs, filmmakers, artists and writers with no real need for imagination, because society has become so numb to anything but the shock factor. It's kind of like splatter films today. Anyone can pour a bucket of fake blood around a set and come up with a gruesome new way to dispatch the morons who never heed the obvious. But a true horror filmmaker, artist, or writer has the ability to instill true fear into their viewers, or readers, and uses the gore only as a supporting cinematic, visual or literary device. The same goes for sex and sensuality in film, art and writing. I think it's way more effective if used as a support to create a mood, rather than an in your face money shot. Okay, I intended that pun. Don't get me wrong, I am by no means a prudish right wing, bible thumper. I just think half the fun of horror and sex in art was in the mystery and having to use your mind to fill in the blanks, rather than have it all spread eagled right there for you, like you're too much of a moron to figure out that part A goes into slot B.

LDP: Do you think comics/graphic novels can ever be taken as a serious art form in the mainstream world of art?

SC: It's kind of like the whole digital art thing. The traditional fine arts community has a very narrow view, at times, of what is defined as viable art. I've always thought it very ironic that the very nature of fine art is pushing the limits of that definition, yet the traditional fine art critics, collectors and curators are mostly conservative in their views on art and very slow to change. That being said though, the other art world, the one you and I reside in, very much think of the graphic novel and comic books as a serious art form. The graphic novel is one of the fastest growing forms of entertainment according to statistics from sources such as ICv2, Diamond and Publishers Weekly. The recession only caused a hiccup in overall sales growth and the advent of electronic devices such as Kindle and Book Nook will only help to bolster sales for both comics and graphic novels as publishers adapt to the technology. A visit to your local comic book shop or bookstore will reveal the amazing level of talent involved in the creation of comics and graphic novels. Starting with the very first credited graphic novel, A Contract with God, by the legendary Will Eisner to groundbreakers such as Berni Wrightson, Vince Locke, Neil Gaiman, Alex Ross and the plethora of modern day talent, it's easy to validate the art of the graphic novel as serious. The same goes for comics. Stan Lee, Jack Kirby, Todd McFarlane, Joe Kubert, Simon Bisley, Glenn Fabry, Neal Adams and the list goes on. The comics and graphic novel industry has always attracted some of the most talented artists to have ever held a pencil.

LDP: Have you ever thought of making a career out of something other than art – if so, then what?

SC: Strangely enough and probably most illustrative of the dichotomy of my psyche, is the pervasive regret at not having made the military a career. I was an infantry sergeant in the US Army and I really loved it. I made sergeant in two years, which isn't easy and I was on the fast track to making it a career. Then Desert Storm happened. My unit was being deactivated as part of President Clinton's big reduction of the military and its budget. What that meant for us, was that we were being plucked up to be assigned as fuel truck drivers (bombs on wheels), mess hall workers, mine field clearing, basically all the jobs an infantry soldier wouldn't want to do. Being a sergeant, I was low on the list, so it'd be a while until they got to me. Someone from headquarters came around asking for volunteers to be chopper gunners and I volunteered with two other buddies.

They turned me down, so they could send me to a unit that needed sergeants, so that it could be deployed to Iraq. Well, it was over by the time the unit was ready and I ended up as a section leader in a platoon with a lieutenant and a company commander that I didn't get along with. On top of that, I was slated to do a hardship tour in Korea, which means you go over alone for 13 months. My youngest daughter had just been born and I would've missed most of her first year of life. It also screwed up my plans on getting into Special Forces. That left a very bad taste in my mouth and I got out. I did reserve drill sergeant for a short time, but it's not the same as active duty. My grandfather was an infantry sergeant during WW II, in the same unit I spent most of my time in, who won a bronze star at the Battle of the Bulge and my father was a Marine during the Vietnam War. A part of me still wishes I could've lived up to that legacy. Antiquated thinking, I know, but it's part of what makes me the perfect tortured artist.

SC: Tattooing is very much like illustration, only your medium is skin. With a tattoo, you have to be able to tell a whole story, or convey a feeling in usually one image, or one big scene, in the case of back pieces and sleeves. I've become very adept at reading someone's rough ideas and turning them into a concrete form. It's become very evident to me, in my work as an illustrator, that I can take the gist of a story, or idea, and narrow it down to a singular, powerful image.

SC: I think I'll continue to tattoo in some capacity. I haven't yet decided what exactly that means, but I will be extremely selective in what I choose to tattoo and my illustration career now comes first. For me, tattooing has been a 20 year detour from my original path in life. When I started on my path to becoming an illustrator 25 years ago, I fell prey to the trappings of youthful thinking and a careless attitude towards my life. I ended up making some bad choices and had to drop out of art school and start working. I started selling cars, where I made even more bad decisions and hung out with people that introduced me to the designer drug of the 80's, cocaine. To make a long story short, I woke up in my car, covered in my own puke and blood, had $500 stolen from me and made a decision at that moment to change my life. That's when the decision to join the Army came about. After I got out, it was too difficult to maintain family obligations, and go to school full time, so I dropped out again. Right at that time, I was offered a tattoo apprenticeship and faced with poverty, or that, I took it. It was never my intent to do it for this long, but it took on a life of its own and the more popular I became, the further away quitting it became.

For me, it's always been about the art, and skin and tattoo ink is just another medium. I'm ready to move onto the next phase of my art career and explore new possibilities of storytelling.

SC: The best way is through my website; atomicdeadguy.com People can see what I do and have access to buy my work, as well as t-shirts and swag through my Artsprojekt and Redbubble stores.

SC: It was a blast, I enjoyed it.

STREET SWEEPING BLUES

by Anthony Giangregorio

Something to make you think . . .

It's 8 a.m. You're warmly snug in bed, dreaming of that next vacation this summer, when suddenly there's a loud voice yelling outside your bedroom window, coming from the street your house is on, waking you like a bomb had gone off. "Please move all cars from the left hand side of such and such a street!"

"Oh, no, the car! It's street sweeping day!" you cry and jump out of bed, throwing on what's near and dashing outside as tow trucks wait to take your car to the impound lot, the prison of modern day vehicles. Why? What did you do to deserve this?

Nothing at all, it's just the annual street sweeping drive to get the streets of your local city clean. So then I ask you, why is it that after the street sweeper flies by my home at running speed, the gutter looks worse that before it came?

Last month my neighbor was going to get towed but he came out just in time. He moved his car and after the sweeper had passed, the sand and refuse was spread out everywhere. It now looked worse than it did before the street sweeper went by. And as I drive around my city on errands, seeing where the sweepers have been, I see the same thing again and again.

And if you're like me, you ask yourself, "What's the point?" That's a very good question. What is the point of having these massive machines with giant brushes zip down our streets and do nothing but make a mess? But don't worry, after it's passed you can always go outside and 'clean' the mess the sweeper made yourself. That seems ridiculous. Oh, wait, I know what you could do if you're really upset. Call the city yard, tell them what's happened, and have them send another sweeper to do the job they were supposed to the first time. What they were 'paid' to do.
Good luck with that, and after that maybe President Obama will come and paint your house. So why is this? Well, I believe it goes way past the sweeping to something in America that to me is becoming a pandemic. We now reward people for doing lousy jobs.

Fifty years ago if you ran your corporate business to the ground, what would happen? You'd lose your company, that's what. Flash forward to 2009-2011. Run your big business to the ground? "Boy that stinks," the government says. "Here, take as much money as you need to get back on your feet, but promise us you'll do better this time. Besides, we don't need all that extra cash, it's just getting under foot anyway."

Here's a better analogy. I took the post office test a few years back. You needed to be there by 8 a.m. So as I got there thirty minutes early, I expected that at 8 a.m. on the dot, the doors would be locked, and if you were late you were out of luck. After all, to let people in after wouldn't be fair to the rest of us who got up early to be there on time. We did what was expected of us as responsible adults.

So what happened at 8 a.m? People were arriving till 8:15 and we all had to wait while they got caught up. Now that's not fair. It seems more and more in this country, the slackers and less motivated are being rewarded, and we are bending over backwards to accommodate them instead of making 'them' aspire to be better than they are. What kind of a future that will bring will be anyone's guess. Not a good one, I bet.

So that's why when the street sweeper flies past our homes once a month and each of us is standing on the sidewalk looking at one another while shaking our heads at the terrible job that's been done, no one does anything, because we as Americans are being brainwashed to think it's okay to be subpar, it's okay to do less than a good job.

Because even if you don't do a good job, the rest of us will just slow down and let you slackers catch up. I guess that's life in 2011. Oh, and if you're wondering how all of this affects my dirty street? Well, I went out and bought a big broom.

THE GUIDE

By Eric S. Brown

George's body lay in the grass. His chest was torn open and a look of stark terror lingered in his lifeless eyes. One of his legs was simply gone.

Richard, Fred, and their guide, Marcus, stood over him. Richard had thrown up when they found the body. He still looked green as he used the back of his hand to wipe away the remaining traces of vomit from his lips.
"You think it was a bear?" Richard asked.

Marcus shook his head. "Doubt it. Ain't no claw marks."

"He was only gone for a few minutes," Fred pointed out. "How could this have happened?"

Marcus shook his head. "This is the woods you're in now, city boys. It ain't never fully safe."

Fred advanced on Marcus, grabbing him by the front of his flannel shirt. "We hired you to come here so we could have a good time. You were supposed to keep us safe!"

"Mister, I've been working in these woods, leading around rich folks like you, for near fifteen years. I ain't never seen nothin' like this, so let go and calm down before I hurt you," Marcus growled.

Fred released him and backed away.

"So what now?" Richard asked. "I mean, how are we going to get his body back to town with us?"

"The closest road is twenty miles from here," Marcus reminded them. "Haulin' him with us is a very bad idea. Not only will it slow us down, but whatever got him may not be done with him yet."

"You're not seriously suggesting we just leave him here, are you?" Fred raged.

Marcus knelt and drew their attention to an indention in the dirt. "See that?" he said. "That belongs to his killer."

The track was huge and shaped like a bare human foot.

"Is that. . ." Richard began but Fred interrupted him.

"Come on! There's no way that's real. You're just messing with us now, aren't you, you bastard?"

"Watch your tongue," Marcus warned him. "I didn't put this print here and your buddy is dead. I strongly suggest we get the hell out of here as fast as we can. I, for one, don't want to meet whatever made this and odds are it'll be back for what's left of him."

Marcus stood up and checked his rifle, making sure the safety was off and that a round was chambered and ready. "This ain't no game anymore and we ain't the hunters either. My guess is we're the hunted now. Keep your eyes and ears open. Follow me and stay close. We ain't stoppin' till we get to the trucks."

"Screw that," Fred said, digging his cell phone from his pocket. He cursed when he saw there was no signal.

"Didn't I tell y'all those didn't work up here?" Marcus said with a smirk.

"Don't you have an emergency radio or something?" Richard asked.

"Nope," Marcus answered. "Never needed one."

"Well, you do now, you hick!" Fred shouted.

Marcus finally broke, losing his usual cool, and punched Fred dead on in the mouth. Fred fell onto his butt and sat there stunned, as blood poured from his lower lip.

He spat a tooth into the grass and looked up at Marcus with a promise of vengeance. "When we get back to civilization, I'm going to sue you into the ground."

Marcus grinned. "Go 'head if you want. Just remember, you ain't home yet and you're not gonna be without me." Stealing a glance at the sky, Marcus sighed. "Daytime's a wastin', boys. We gotta get movin'."

An hour later, they were still walking south through the trees. Fred was so exhausted he appeared to be on the verge of collapse. There had been no sign of whatever it was that killed George, but still Marcus seemed spooked.

"What is it?" Richard asked him quietly.

"It's here." Marcus unsung his rifle from his shoulder. "I can feel it."

"Great," Fred said, panting and pausing to lean against the closest tree. "Our guide, the Jedi. Thank God, he's so in touch with the forest."

"Shut up," Marcus whispered.

Without warning, a giant, hulking creature stepped from the trees a few feet behind them. It stood nearly ten feet tall, all muscle and hair. Its yellow eyes burned with a deep, feral rage as it stared at them.

"Holy. . ." Marcus breathed, not believing his eyes as all hell broke loose and the beast sprang at them.

Fred didn't even have time to react as it hefted him effortlessly into the air, snapping his spine like a twig. Richard fumbled with his weapon, desperately trying to ready it, as he lost control of his bladder and the front of his pants grew wet.

Marcus' .30-.06 cracked as the beast flung Fred's corpse aside. The high-powered round slammed into the beast's side with a bright-red spray of blood as it entered its flesh. The beast stopped, pressing a huge, human-like hand over the wound.

It turned toward Marcus with a roar and he fired again. This time, the beast's head flew back as the shot smacked into the center of its forehead. Its massive body reeled about and collapsed into a heap on the forest floor.

"You killed it," Richard said in awe.

"I sure did." Marcus chambered another round. "Gonna be rich too," he laughed.

"What? Wait!" Richard squealed as Marcus raised his rifle once more.

"It's my kill and I ain't sharin' it with anyone."

The crack of the rifle echoed in the trees and Richard's brain matter was splattered all over the tree behind him. Marcus calmly walked over to the Sasquatch's body, already trying to figure out a way to move it. Not only was he going to be rich, but he was going to be famous, too.

"Stupid city boys," he snorted. This trip had turned out to be a good one after all. At least for him.

The Corn Has Eyes

by Dane T. Hatchell

The sun broke over the eastern horizon, casting an orange glow on Reverend Flake's small farm. The air was thick with moisture; dew glistened on the grass and weeds grew in the crop fields. The nocturnal animals scurried to find refuge for their daytime rest. The reverend started his daily chores well before sunup, sitting on an old wooden stool, squeezing out milk from his two cows into a metal bucket. After the cows were watered and fed, he moved over to the chicken shack for the ritual egg gathering before having breakfast with his wife and daughter. When the sun rose high enough for his tired old eyes to see, he hooked the yoke to his loyal mule and plow. With the snap of the bridle reins, the mule began its walk, turning the soil for the spring crops. Reverend Flake's only son was serving in the Army, fighting Hitler in Germany. Several members of his flock pledged the day before to come by and give him a hand. It was a daunting task for one man to take alone. But not one of the well intended had shown. He was disappointed, but understood. Their farms and families came first. In his heart, he felt that God would provide. When the time was right, He always provided. The earth gave way under the heavy iron plow, turning clumps of grass roots to the sky, and sending worms and insects scurrying from the light of day. Sweat formed on his brow as the day heated, and stung his eyes as the salt and grime trickled down from his forehead. As he stood a moment to wipe his face with his handkerchief, his eyes focused on a man approaching from down the road, a sack slung over his shoulder. He squinted, and shielded the sun with his forearm. This man wasn't one of his parishioners; in fact, he didn't recognize him at all. A tall young man with broad shoulders greeted the reverend with a cheerful smile, "Mornin', sir, my name's Pickings, James Pickings. They call me Jim." He removed the straw hat from his head and held it to his chest. The two shook hands, the reverend could see the man's bulging biceps through his worn flannel shirt. "Good to meet you, Jim. I'm Reverend Flake, Reverend James Flake. I guess we got the same Christian name. Now, what brings you here, boy?"
"Well, sir, I'm working my way down south. I hear they need some help down there in the oil fields. I'm looking to go down there for some steady work," Jim said with a gleam in his bright blue eyes. "Sir, I'll give you a day's hard work if you can feed me and put me up for the night. You don't have to pay me or nothing. I'll be on my way first thing tomorrow. Once I get to town, I figure I can hitch a ride." "Son, you don't know it, but you're the answer to my prayers." The reverend slapped him on the arm. "You help me get my crops planted, and I'll make things right for you." Jim walked past the reverend and grabbed the handles to the plow. He put his bottom lip under his teeth and made a whistle that startled the mule from its rest, and sent it plodding forward again. The reverend retrieved a bag of corn from the barn and started planting in the newly tilled soil. As the hours passed, the morning gave way to noon. Without much enticement, the reverend convinced Jim it was time to rest a spell, and break for lunch. Back at the farmhouse, the two left their dirt encased boots on the front porch, and met the others in the kitchen. "This here is my wife Edna, and that there's my daughter, Elisa," the reverend said. Both of the women gave their cordial hellos. Jim politely returned the greeting. His eyes fixated on Elisa, not sparing more than half a second glance at Edna. He was so enchanted that a shotgun could have been fired by his head and it would have gone unnoticed. Elisa was dressed in a sheer white blouse that contoured to her ample bosoms. Her aging denim skirt hung well above her knees, exposing her long legs, firm calves, and perfect feet. The reverend closed one eye and raised one brow; this boy was just like all the others, smitten by the sin of lust for his daughter. The three sat down to a lunch of ham and biscuits, with fig preserves on the side, and washed it down with cold milk. Jim dominated the conversation, asking three questions for every one asked of him.

Jim's eyes darted around the room as he spoke. The reverend found his shiftiness curious, but excused it for the man being nervous around Elisa. Eventually, Jim calmed down and relaxed. But unknown to the reverend and his family, Jim was looking for something in particular; something that most people had in their kitchen. A jar, a special jar. A jar that contained cash money. Jim finally spotted it in a corner of a top shelf, behind a ceramic rooster. The rooster had dried butter beans glued to it to look like feathers. There were other odd knick-knacks made from vegetables in the kitchen and throughout the house. After lunch, Jim inquired about them. "Oh, that's Elisa's art. She uses vegetables from the garden. See that picture right there?" the reverend pointed to a wall in the living room. "The cows, the pasture, the whole picture, all made from beans." Jim walked up to the picture, and sure enough, Elisa had glued hundreds of painted beans to a canvas, producing a somewhat realistic scene. "She sure is talented," Jim said. "As talented as she is pretty." The reverend pulled Jim aside and whispered, "Look son, don't be getting too close to her. She looks sweet and innocent. But she's unstable, you know what I mean?" Jim stared back blankly. No, he didn't know what the reverend meant, and figured it was just a father's way to scare him away from his daughter. "Don't doubt me, boy, she'll hurt you. You do as I say. Now, let's get back to work, daylight's burning." Jim had hurt a few young girls along the way in his lifetime, a few wives, too, all with broken hearts. He knew better than to let the tables turn on him. The day melted into evening, and the evening to night. The two men retired from the field, and the four shared supper together. They passed the night with story telling, until the tiredness of the day set in. Jim was given the room attached to the woodshed to bed down. Edna provided him with clean sheets, a pillow, and a blanket for a comfortable stay. While he was preparing his bed, through his window he could see Elisa standing at her window, looking up into the sky at the full moon. Her long blond hair covered her left bosom and he swore he could see the naked image of her right breast through her thin nightgown. Outside, the water pump for the well was in front of his room, and a towel and bar of soap he found in a chest-of-drawers gave him an idea. He was going to set a trap, and make himself the bait. Off came his shirt to the floor, followed by his pants and underwear, and went outside and posed by the pump. Pretending he wasn't aware of her, he pumped a pail full of well water, dipped the soap in it, and lathered up in the cool night air. The moonlight glistened off his bare chest, as he flexed and tightened his muscles to work out the soreness of the day. He chanced a peek toward Elisa's window, and was surprised to see she was no longer there. He didn't know if he embarrassed her, or if his plan had worked and she was sneaking outside to see him. Thoughts that she might have gone to tell the reverend that he was acting lewdly outside her window made him worry that he'd acted hastily. He realized he needed to stop listening to the little head between his legs, and needed to forget about the young woman and just to take the money and run. Jim dried off and returned to his room, blew the candle out, and lay in bed. Elisa never showed up, but thankfully, neither did the reverend. It was too early to execute his plan to take the cash, so he closed his eyes, and drifted off to sleep. He awoke to the sound of crickets chirping, and looked at his watch. It was after two in the morning and it was time to make his move. Getting dressed and moving as stealthily as possible across the yard, he entered the kitchen through the back door. The old wooden floors creaked beneath his feet. Ever so slowly he walked, step by step, until he reached the corner, and stood on his toes to get the jar behind the ceramic rooster. The metal top scraped against the grooves of the painted glass as he twisted it off. The scraping noise was amplified by the calmness of the night. He resumed his task more slowly, until the lid came off in his hand. In all, he counted over eighty dollars in the jar, the life savings of the humble reverend. Placing the jar back on the shelf, he was nearly to the door when he heard Elisa whisper his name. Jim froze in his tracks, his mind racing. He turned to see her holding a candle not ten feet away.

"Oh, hi there, Elisa," he said softly. "I...I couldn't sleep, so I came for a glass of milk." She turned her head to the side. "I'll get you one." Seeing her voluptuous figure pressing against her nightgown made the little head in his pants once again influence his better judgment. "Say, get yourself one too, and we'll have it outside under the stars." After she poured the milk, the two strolled outside. Jim leaned close to Elisa's side, then slid an arm around her waist, letting his hand come to rest on her hip. "Are you happy here? Living with your Ma and Pa?" Jim asked. "Why wouldn't I be happy?" she asked. "Well, life on a farm can be hard. You ever get a hankering to go to the big city? Maybe you could go to Hollywood. You're pretty, you could be a star," Jim said. "Hollywood's sin city my Pa says. Only a Jezebel would parade herself that way across the big screen." Jim finished his milk, took Elisa's glass from her hand, and set both on the ground. "Why don't you come away with me? I ain't going to Hollywood; I'm going down south to work. You could come with me. We could get married and have children." "Pa says I can't get married. He says I'm cursed, and that I've got to live out here on the farm for the rest of my days," Elisa said without emotion. "Cursed? Why, the only curse I see is that he's got you hoodwinked on stayin' here. You're young and beautiful. You need to leave your parents, just like Adam and Eve's kids left them. Be fruitful and multiply, or somethin' like that." "You shouldn't be talking such nonsense," Elisa frowned. "That's the Devil talking." "The Devil talking? Why, I tell you what, I saw you looking at me when I was bathing earlier. You liked what you saw, I know you did. I know women, and I know you want me." Elisa took a step back. "Jim! What kind of girl do you think I am?" He stepped toward her, and looked at her face to face. "I can see with my own two eyes what kind of girl you are. Now, why don't you come on into my room? I can make you feel real good." Elisa shook her head. "Pa says, if thy eye offends you, pluck it out." She reached in a pocket of her nightgown, and pulled out a kitchen knife. Jim's face lit up in surprise as the moonlight reflected off the blade. She thrust it up under his left eye, and into his brain. "What are you making there, sweetheart?" the Reverend asked Elisa, as she was working on a project at the kitchen table. "I'm making a jacket for my People-corn," she said, tying a knot in the last stitch and biting it in two. "There, I'm finished." "People-corn, what's that?" he asked. She got up from the table and went to the kitchen sink. An ear of corn lay on a towel next to it, a small pair of pants wrapped on the bottom end. With her back to her father, she put the jacket around the mid-section, then straightened out the clothing. "There, it's finished. What do you think? Ain't he pretty?" She turned around and held the People-corn for him to see. Adorned to look like a miniature human, the ear of corn was complete with two of the bluest human eyes pinned to the top end, just under a tiny straw hat. The reverend shook his head and said rhetorically yet sadly, "I warned that boy." Working the field would have to wait, he had another grave to dig.

Shock Waves

Reviewed by Tony Schaab

A lot of movie genres have what folks call "sub-genres," where you can find more specialized types of tales within the greater grouping. The horror genre is a unique area of film-making, because even the horror sub-genres have sub-genres of their own! Within the realm of horror films, one of the hottest sub-genres right now is, of course, stories about zombies. But even within this grouping, many sub-sub-genres exist: you've got your zombie comedy, fast-zombie stories, zombie romances, infection-style zombies…the list could go on for quite some time. In my opinion, one of the quirkiest ones on the list easily has to be the sub-sub-genre for Nazi zombies. It's such an odd pairing, like chocolate and oranges, but always seems to work very well together! The entrants into this sub-sub-genre are surprisingly plentiful in number: you can easily find films like "Dead Snow," "Zombie Lake," "Night of the Zombies," "Horrors of War," "Oasis of the Zombies," "Outpost," and the list goes on. But we must give credit where credit is due, and there is one film that truly started the zombie Nazi-sploitation movement: 1977's "Shock Waves." (Some may argue that 1967's "The Frozen Dead" was the first, but that film features semi-zombie bio-engineered monsters, at best).

"Shock Waves" is an enjoyable entry into the zombie universe, even if it is often overlooked by fans or not even known about at all. In it, Peter Cushing stars as a "retired" Nazi Commander living "mostly" alone on an island off the coast of Florida. When a group of shipwrecked divers come ashore and start poking around where they shouldn't, trouble (for them) ensues. In a case of either smelling out new prey or just really bad timing, a squad of Nazi Zombies known as The Death Corps, who have been living under the sea for the last few decades, decide to head ashore and partake in some good old-fashioned flesh-eating mayhem.

The zombies featured in this film are a unique-looking bunch: they are green and scaly, possibly a side-effect of living underwater for so long, and they all wear odd-looking black goggles that obscure their eyes. In all honesty, the goggles were probably added to the monsters' get-ups more for practicality than anything else, as the zombies (and the actors who play them) spend a fair amount of time ambling around the ocean floor. Although it appears there is an entire squad of at least twenty-plus of the undead, the zombies were actually all played by only eight different actors. Although they may not look particularly scary in relation to some of the living dead in other films, the scenes of them all slowly rising as one out of the water is quite chilling, and to me is one of the most iconic zombie video moments of all time.

Of course, the film featured actors other than the undead, and the viewer is treated to a definite bonus of Peter Cushing hamming it up with full gusto. He and co-star John Carradine each worked only four days on the film – "Shock Waves" took a total of 25 days to shoot – and were each paid

$5,000 for their time. A largely-unknown cast rounded out the rest of the production. Director Ken Weiderhorn would go on to languish in relative obscurity, helming such forgettable films as "Meatballs II" and "A House in the Hills," although it is worth noting he did direct another zombie film, 1988's "Return of the Living Dead Part II." Much of the film takes place inside an abandoned hotel on the island, in which Cushing's SS Commandant has taken up residence. The hotel featured is an actual Biltmore hotel in Florida; it was shut down for a two-year period and abandoned at the time of filming. Weiderhorn paid $250 to rent the building for the shoot. In an amusing twist of fate, the hotel was actually renovated a couple of years after the film shot there, and each room now costs significantly more than $250 per night! Astute viewers will also notice the wrecked ship used in the background of many sea and shore shots. In real-life, this vessel is the S.S. Sapona, a concrete-hulled cargo steamer that ran aground near the Bahamian island of Bimini during a hurricane in 1926. The ship remains at this location to this day, and serves as both a navigational landmark for boaters and as a popular recreational dive site. When you get right down to it, "Shock Waves" doesn't exactly break any molds or change the face of cinema forever, but it definitely has its place in zombie-movie history. It's quite an original take on the genre, with some very interesting ideas being tossed around. The film is definitely worth a watch, especially to those of you who consider yourselves true zombie fans.

Tony Schaab is the author of Reviews of the Dead and The Gore Score Volumes 1 & 2.

Hardware

Reviewed by Tony Schaab

Yes, it's a relatively obscure film from the early 1990s. However, those that overlook "Hardware" as just another robot-gone-mad sci-fi movie are missing out on one of the most stylized and subtly frightening stories of its time. "Hardware" tells the tale of Moses, a mercenary-type scavenger living in a post-apocalyptic world in which most of the Earth has been turned into a radioactive wasteland. In an attempt to bring something unique home to his artsy girlfriend Jill, he buys a bag of broken-down cyborg parts from a wandering nomad and gives it to Jill for her to use in her sculpting. Little does either of them realize that the seemingly-random collection of parts includes the still-active mainframe of a M.A.R.K.-13, a government project to create a self-sustaining robotic killing machine. Soon the M.A.R.K.-13 has not only begun to rebuild itself inside of Jill's apartment, but it's also looking to fulfill its primary directive: kill, kill, kill! The movie is "inspired by" a comic strip from the popular British sci-fi variety magazine called 2000AD, a periodical most known for being the genesis of Judge Dredd. The comic that inspired the film, "SHOK!," took place with the cyborg head being recovered from the Cursed Earth, the barren post-apocalyptic landscape from the Judge Dredd universe. Even though the film heavily references the storyline of the comic, no mention was made of the connection during the marketing and theatrical run of "Hardware."

Obviously, this caused a bit of a stir with the 2000AD folks. Following legal action on their part, the film now sports a "Based on" notice in the credits, as well as full writing credit being given to the creators of "SHOK!," Steve McManus and Kevin O'Neill. "Hardware" is now considered by most to be the first "official" movie spin-off from a 2000AD story. As for the film itself, it's an incredibly smart story that blends sci-fi and horror together very seamlessly. It's even more impressive when you realize that the film was made in the early 1990s, a time when both science fiction and horror were particularly hard sells to movie-going audiences. The film is notable for the appearance of Dylan McDermott in the lead role of Moses, long before he found fame on television in "The Practice" or was named to People's "Most Beautiful People" lists in 1998 and 2000. Stacey Travis stars as the feisty red-headed Jill, and it's truly a shock to me that this stunning beauty never went on to a much bigger Hollywood career. Also of note in the casting department are small roles for musicians Lemmy (from the rock group Motörhead) as a cab driver and Iggy Pop as a radio DJ that is heard on-air in Jill's apartment. Much of the plot is spent focused on the self-repairing robotic monstrosity stalking and maiming Jill, along with Moses and other characters who were unfortunate enough to enter Jill's apartment. There are some very interesting graphical representations in the film, including the "Matrix-esque" green-tinged computer modules and the fashion in which the M.A.R.K.-13 incorporates any and all pieces of technology into its physical rebuilding process. It's an approach one might explain as a "techno smorgasbord!"

As the cyborg continues to grow and become stronger, measures become increasingly desperate for would-be hero Moses and his supporting cast. The film culminates in an ending that is an existential and trippy mind-bender that may best be described as "The Ten Commandments" meets "2001: A Space Odyssey." An odd pairing, to be sure, but religious elements are actually sprinkled throughout the film. Some of the prime examples are McDermott's character's name of Moses and the M.A.R.K.-13 itself: in the Bible, the book of Mark, Chapter 13 concludes with the phrase "No flesh shall be spared." It's one of the most interesting and head-scratching conclusions to a film I have ever witnessed. Quite frankly, you have to see it to believe it. "Hardware" was not well-received by critics during its theatrical run. While Fangoria magazine called it "the best science-fiction thriller since "Alien," Entertainment Weekly gave the film a grade of D+, calling it unoriginal and going so far as to say that it was "as if someone had remade Alien with the monster played by a rusty erector set." Apparently in 1990, all the critics had to compare films to was "Alien!" Despite the mixed reviews, the film has gone on to gain a cult following on home video, largely due to its unique telling of a truly frightening post-apocalyptic tale. Director Richard Stanley actually wrote a sequel to the film, which he titled "Hardware II: Ground Zero." The film reportedly would have been different in scope than the original, utilizing more elements from the Western genre, and would have featured a much grander scale of story. After trying for a few years without success to find a studio for the film, the idea was ultimately scrapped, due in part to the fact that the rights to the original movie are split between several parties. This certainly doesn't detract from the fact that "Hardware" is a singular viewing experience, and one I can highly recommend to serious fans of sci-fi and horror alike.

Tony Schaab is the author of *Reviews of the Dead* and *The Gore Score Volumes 1 & 2*.

A SERBIAN FILM reviewed by Kelly Hudson

This is without a doubt the most disturbing film I've ever seen. The movie has made its way through the festival circuits and stirred-up outrage and debate wherever the film has been shown, and for good reason. This is combative cinema. Milos, a retired porn star in Serbia, is lured into one last job. The money he saved is running out just when he needs it to help support schooling for his young son and the daily costs of living with his wife. The job offer comes from a former associate of his who has gone on to star in animal porn and if this isn't a tip-off that things are going to get strange, then I guess nothing else could be. The man Milos goes to work for has an idea of mixing art with porn but he wants to keep his star in the dark as to the plot. Milos gets offered a bundle of money, too much to turn down despite his misgivings, and finds himself drawn into an increasingly tightening circle of hell itself. After some uncomfortable encounters that flirt with child porn and indulges in masochism, Milos decides to back out. But it's too late now as things rapidly fly out of control. And then there's the "Newborn Porn" scene, and you're either vomiting or running for the exit. From there, it's a descent into madness and depravity and the movie becomes an endurance test. Can you make it through to the end, to discover, along with Milos, just what evil he's participated in? You see, Milos gets dosed continuously with a mixture of animal "Viagra" and speed, so he's out of his mind with lust and violence. It's a white-knuckle ride to the end and after it's over, Milos and his family will never be the same. Neither will you. I know it really disturbed me, and I think I got the point. Here's this country, scarred by war and ethnic cleansing, where life has been reduced to the ridiculous. Normal people, working class folks like Milos (even though he works with his dick, he's an artist, no more different than a master electrician or a plumber) have their lives ripped from them and are forced to participate in things so terrible there is no coming back from them. No, there is no war mentioned in the film and it doesn't involve any soldiers. Instead, I believe, this film shows the effects of dehumanizing war and what it does to the common people. They, like Milos, get dragged into involvement with things they'd never conceive as possible and when they find out what they've done, they have to deal with the consequences. Watch this only if you have a strong stomach and can put your moral objections aside. Whether you do or don't, you will still be left sick, dizzy, and furious. This film is no joke; it's the real deal. It forces each viewer to confront things they most probably never wished to deal with. You've been warned.

La Horde reviewed by Kelly Hudson

In a world full of zombie movies and the increasingly awesome Walking Dead TV show, how does this French film stack up to the litany of living dead stories already available? Well, pretty good. A group of crooked cops break into an abandoned tenement building where, all the way upstairs, a group of Nigerian criminals are holed up. The cops move in to assassinate the criminals but fail, getting half of their crew killed and the rest captured. And just as the criminals are about to put the finishing touches on the survivors, the zombie apocalypse comes down. What follows is a series of frayed allegiances and betrayals and a whole bunch of blood. "La Horde" is pretty much a zombie film stripped down to its very core: a group of survivors must fight their way free of an infested building to hopefully reach safety outside, even as the world around them falls apart. Every corner turned could be a death sentence, and as they try desperately to stay alive, each step leads them into twisting passages of terror, and for some, death. There's nothing new here, nothing unique explored about the characters or the zombies, but it's a lean, mean, thrilling machine. There are a couple of highlights that really stood out amidst the carnage: first off, the cop who gets surrounded by a horde of the living dead as he stands atop a car roof. He knows he's a dead man and yet he goes down fighting in the most spectacular way, first using his guns, then his machete, and finally his fists and feet. It's pretty awesome. And the second is one I don't want to spoil too much, but let's say it involves a giant machine gun and a corridor full of zombies. If you like zombie flicks and want some good popcorn splatter, this is the movie for you. The last thirty minutes are nothing but pure terror and if that's your cup of tea, then pull up a chair and sit right down. You've just come home.

Desire of Flesh by Nelia Thompson

Susan waited expectantly for Bill to get home, laying on the bed wearing exactly what he liked–the black lace bra, with matching thong, and the thigh-high-sheer-stockings and garter belt he'd given her last month for Christmas. She shivered and thought about covering up with a blanket, but she knew she would get punished if she did, though the thought of a spanking was sounding really good right then. He was late and she was already horny. As she thought about masturbating, she finally heard the front door bang open, making her jump and then tingle with excitement at what she knew was coming. Heavy foot falls came down the hall, slow and plodding. She shivered and wiggled in anticipation as she saw the door knob turning. Susan expected to see her husband Bill standing in the doorway, looking her over with hungry appreciation. What she got was an undead version of her husband looking her over like she was a steak. Bill must have died while on his way home, and from the looks of his erection, he'd been thinking about her when he'd passed. Susan bit her lip. Should she or shouldn't she? Bill moved toward the bed, shuffling and moaning. Susan sat up and undid his belt buckle when he reached her. As she gently tugged down his pants, she moaned, "God, you're hard," while stroking his cock and sucking the tip. Bill just watched her and moaned, a somewhat confused expression in his eyes. "I want you," she said, standing and sliding off her thong. She'd put them on after the stockings, like he liked. He loved fucking her while she wore the stockings. Turning around, Susan got down on her hands and knees on the bed. She reached back between her legs and guided his cold, ridged cock into her hot, wet, throbbing pussy. The temperature and texture of him excited her in ways she'd never experienced before. Groaning, she thrust her hips back against him, fucking him hard and fast. Bill just stood there, moaning like the zombie he was. As Susan reached her climax, she screamed and thrust against him harder. All of a sudden she felt a snap. She turned around, his cock still inside her. "Oh, no," she whimpered. "I broke it off. I'm so sorry." Hurriedly, she pulled his cock out of her pussy and tried to figure out how they could reattach it. Looking up at him, she realized he was very angry. "I didn't mean to break it," she said, frantically trying to get it to stick back on, like his blood should be glue. Bill moaned angrily and grabbed her by the neck. Holding her there, he knelt down between her legs, pushing them apart. He leaned forward, grunting and moaning as he sucked and licked her pussy. Susan moaned and spread her legs further for him, gasping as he gripped her neck tighter in his excitement. Unexpectedly, Bill bit off a chunk of hot, wet flesh and ate it.

Susan screamed in pain and tried to close her legs and dislodge his grip on her throat, but he was too strong. He squeezed her throat harder the more she fought, biting, chewing, and swallowing the softest, sweetest part of her body. After he removed most of the flesh, he sucked at the blood gushing from her body. With one last whimper, Susan passed out. Soon, she bled to death. Twenty minutes later, she woke up, found his detached cock on the bed and started eating it, while Bill continued to eat her crotch. They spent the night devouring and enjoying each other carnally. By morning, there wasn't much left of either of them. They'd fulfilled every desire of their flesh.

Who knew that living to see tomorrow would involve lying face down in the mud, sucking air through a reed? Jeff Monroe thought, doing just that. He couldn't believe that just a month ago, his life had been normal. He'd been a normal guy with a family. Now it was all gone. The 'Beings' had come. There wasn't another name for them, because no one knew who the Beings were or where they came from. The closest thing that came to mind for Jeff was mutants. But that would mean they'd been human to begin with and he didn't think they were. He had joined the Rebels to fight the Beings after they'd eaten his daughter and kidnapped his wife. Now . . . he could hear them coming. They were behind him, on the right. They'd almost passed him by, when one stepped directly in the center of his lower back. Its clawed foot dug into his flesh and curled around his spinal cord. Jeff screamed. The Being stepped off him and signaled to the others with a chirping noise. They gathered around while Jeff was lifted into the air by his neck. Realizing he could no longer move the lower half of his body, he knew he had no chance. Even if he managed to get free, he couldn't escape. He noticed three other Rebels had also been captured. They were bound together to form a chain gang, managed by another Being wearing a black cloak. Jeff knew they would be taken to the Hall of Twelve, and it was more than likely t hey would all die there. During the journey, he passed out from pain. When Jeff regained consciousness, he found himself lying in the corner of a poorly lit, dingy room. He counted twenty captives, including himself. A Being in a black cloak sat behind a small, square table under the only light in the room, a bare bulb hanging from wires. Jeff winced and pulled himself upright. Another of the Beings entered through a steel door. It buzzed and clicked something to the one behind the table, receiving a nod in response. The new arrival grabbed a man and dragged him over to the table. The sitting Being nudged a pair of red dice toward the man. Jeff remembered the crazy man they'd found in the woods. He'd told them of the Hall of Twelve—about the roll of the dice, and freedom or death. Only one number would set you free, the rest would decide which room, and which horror, would be your death. The crazy man's roll had gained him his freedom. The man picked up the dice and rolled. The Beings squealed with delight and the man was dragged through the steel door. His begging echoed back as he was dragged down a long hallway. Strange growls, howls, and roaring bellowed out as well. Moments later, the man screamed in terror and pain. The remaining captives shuddered, and one man started to cry and blubber pathetically. Tears came to Jeff's eyes as well, but not from fear. He felt like a failure. He would never find his wife and save her. The next man chosen walked up to the table with his head held high. He picked up the dice and tossed them down on the table with disgust.

The Beings hissed. The man was shoved toward a small wooden door in the opposite wall of the metal one. As it was opened, the sun shown in, birds chirped, and the smell of grass floated on the air. The man was shoved out and the door was slammed closed. The captives began to stir, one man tried to get closer to the table to see what had been rolled. He was pushed back immediately. The 'handler' Being moved to grab someone else from the crowd, but the one at the table made rapid clicking noises and nodded at Jeff. The handler complied and picked Jeff up, bringing him to the table. Jeff was shaking. His nerves were stretched so tautly between fear and hope that he didn't know what to do or think. He rolled. The dice rattled on the table and bumped against the one inch wooden lip. Six . . . he'd rolled a six, and as the Beings made sounds of pleasure, he knew he was doomed. Jeff was carried to the metal door and thrust through. The growls, howls, and roaring began anew, now more spine tingling in the hall than they'd been in the waiting room. Each creature was hidden in a room with a steel door. Blood was gushing out from under door number two. Must have been the first man, he thought. He shook harder as he passed each door. When he was before door number six, the Being slid back the metal bar and opened it. Jeff was so scared he was clutching the cloak the Being was wearing. But with a quick yank, he was torn off and thrown into the pitch black room. The door slammed closed behind him and was re-bolted. He heard a long, low growl from the far corner of the room and he peed himself. He felt something move and bump into his limp legs. Blinding pain shot up his arm as something bit him and tore off his forearm. The pain was overwhelming, his screams deafening. Again a bite, and the rest of his left arm was ripped off with violent tugging and jerking. Jeff was in so much pain he could no longer scream. He lay gasping for breath, each attempt for air a spasm of tortured pain. His right arm received the same treatment, then his legs were ripped off. As he lay there, nothing more than a torso with a head, he gasped his last breath with an image of his beautiful wife flashing through his mind. "I'm sorry," he breathed as unseen jaws clamped down on his face, crushing his skull and ending his life.

Interview with
NICK CATO

LDP: Please tell us a little bit about yourself and how you came to be a writer –

NC: I've always been a major fan of horror, be it by films, comics, or books. I started reading before I was out of kindergarten, and always loved to read (I now average about 75 novels a year). While I thought music was going to be my thing (I played drums in several bands—of different styles—from around 1983-1991), I became sick and tired of gigging, and several years after I was married (in 1991), I began to try my hand at writing. I started taking it seriously around 1999-2000, although before that I had published and reviewed films in some crudely-done fanzines.

LDP: What are the titles of your books?

NC: DON OF THE DEAD (2009 Coscom Entertainment) was my debut novel. I'm currently shopping my second one (tentatively titled SUBURBAN EXORCIST) and am about halfway done writing my third. I also currently have a novella titled THE APOCALYPSE OF PETER being considered by 2 publishers.

LDP: What are your books about?

NC: DON OF THE DEAD is basically a dark comedy/horror yarn that's a blend of THE GODFATHER and DAWN OF THE DEAD. I had started writing it around 2000, but put it on the back burner for a few years as I began to sell short stories to online e-zines and a few horror magazines and anthologies. I think it's a fun read and I was thrilled to receive some glowing reviews from several authors I highly respect.

SUBURBAN EXORCIST is (guess what?) a riff on THE EXORCIST, as well as ecumenism. I think it's a funny one, although it takes a strange turn toward the ending.

THE APOCALYPSE OF PETER is an end-times tale that DOESN'T feature zombies. I tried to create a unique look at the end of the world as seen through the eyes of a young seminary student and a tough old man. It's borderline bizarre and I had a blast writing it.

LDP: What do you think people would like about your book and why?

NC: I wrote DON to move quickly: there's very little (if any) stalling. In fact a few people have told me what they liked best about it is how the novel begins right in the center of the action and how the short chapters make it difficult to put it down.

LDP: Have you had any other publications? If so, where?

NC: My first professional sale was to an anthology titled DEATHGRIP: EXIT LAUGHING (2006 Hellbound Books). There were a lot of authors featured in this thick paperback, but I was beyond thrilled to have my first pro-published story alongside one of my all-time favorite writers, the legendary William Nolan. I've also had stories in several other anthologies, the latest being in last year's HOUDINI GUT PUNCH, a Bizarro-horror anthology from Library of the Living Dead Press. It's great to see the Bizarro genre gaining popularity; I've always been a fan of weird films and literature, so it's great to see this stuff finally finding a larger audience.

LDP: What inspires you as a writer?

NC: Mainly the low-budget exploitation films I grew up on. I always was and always will be a fan of serious horror, but horror comedies (as well as unusual B-movies) have a special place in my life that I can't explain without sounding like I need to be institutionalized.

LDP: Who's your favorite author?

NC: Nearly impossible to pin it down to one, but suffice it to say, although I grew up on King and Koontz (like nearly every other writer in this genre), it wasn't until I read Richard Laymon's novel, NIGHT SHOW, in 1987, that I had a desire to write. He had a style that was cinematic and always exciting. This book struck a chord in me.

Today I rarely miss anything by Gary A. Braunbeck and Tom Piccirilli. There's plenty of others I follow, but I consider these two among the best and most consistent writers of dark fiction today.

LDP: What's your favorite genre to read?

NC: Horror. I read a lot of Bizarro, science fiction, and the occasional literary novel (not to mention a lot of non-fiction), but I always find myself looking forward to the next horror novel on my To-Be-Read pile.

LDP: What's your favorite genre to write?

NC: While not technically a genre, I always find my stories (even most of the ones I start out being serious with) taking silly or really offbeat turns. Horror/comedy hybrids are my passion, although lately I've been writing a lot of strange stuff that easily fits into the Bizarro category.

I'm also currently reviewing books and films for 4 different websites, and am working on a non-fiction book about unusual cult films with another writer. I find writing about and reviewing films/books helps me warm up to my fiction writing.

LDP: What advice do you have for any aspiring writers?

NC: Ignore anyone who wants to pull you down, whether intentionally or not. After my first novel was published, I shared an idea for my second novel with a writer friend who insisted I'd never be able to make (said idea) novel-length. Yet I finished the novel in almost half the time it took me to write DON OF THE DEAD.

If you have the bug to write something, write and write until it's done, THEN see what others think about it (if you feel the need to coincide with someone). At least that has been working for me (even with my short stories).

LDP: Your book DON OF THE DEAD is a fresh take on zombies, how did the concept for the novel come about exactly?

NC: DON OF THE DEAD is a combo of my two favorite film genres: horror and gangster. I grew up as much with THE GODFATHER as I did with NIGHT OF THE LIVING DEAD, so when I was toying with ideas for a first novel, the name DON OF THE DEAD popped into my head (of course, a riff on DAWN OF THE DEAD). It was a culmination of all these films I watched religiously while growing up.

I remember when I was nearly done writing it, there was a paranormal romance with the same title that had been published—and I wanted to scream! Yet it's so different from my story I managed to get over it (during a google search, I even found out there's a singer for some death metal band who goes by the name DON OF THE DEAD—so I quickly learned not to get too attached to titles).

LDP: Of all the characters in your story, which is your favorite and why?

NC: I'd have to go with Father Sergio. He's a Catholic priest who holds a dark secret yet for some reason has no fear of the zombies. Every time he came into the story I had a great time creating his antics, and I had an even better time coming up with his demise.

Too bad he's dead—I could've probably written another novel just based around him (and I'm not too big on prequels, so please, no requests!).

LDP: Have you ever co-written anything with another author? If so, was it a pleasant experience?

NC: I co-wrote a novella with author L.L. Soares, but we still haven't had it edited. We're both huge fans of 70s grindhouse films, so we decided to write a story that was a cross between BLOODSUCKING FREAKS, the Dirty Harry films, and we even threw some "blaxploitation" in for good measure. Maybe we'll get some lunatic to tinker with it for us one day, but for now we've both been quite busy with other projects. It was pleasant working with L.L., although I'm assuming a 20k novella is a lot easier to do than an 85K novel.

LDP: Of everything you've ever written, what was your favorite?

NC: My favorite is a short story titled I BURIED A FERGASON (a.k.a. ZOMBIE VIII in ITALY), which was published in the 2007 anthology, 'Southern Fried Weirdness Volume One' by SFW Press. I took the zombie thing and really twisted it, adding a redneck cast, an obscure virus, and a possessed toilet bowl. I'm hoping a lot more people will get to read it if I ever sell my first short story collection (which, BTW, I'm almost done compiling).

LDP: Do you have any tips on editing that you would like to share?

NC: Whether you're editing your own work or someone else's, read THE ENTIRE STORY aloud. Tom Monteleone gives this tip all the time, and he gave it to me back at the World Horror Convention in NY in 2005. It's amazing how many simple errors you find when you read stories aloud. It's a priceless practice to get into.

LDP: What are your pet peeves or 'issues' with grammar?

NC: My only pet peeve is when people use the term "Thank you very much" as a retort or sarcastic come-back. It was cool to do about 7 years ago, but when I see it today I want to scream. It's played out, it sounds silly, and it's just not cool anymore. I find this term all the time even in novels from some of my favorite authors. PLEASE STOP THIS INSANITY. Thanks.

Also, in a lot of novels I review by first time authors, there is an over abundance (especially among the self-published crowd) of the word 'THAT.' It's a basic mistake everyone makes, yet one that needs to be dealt with, ESPECIALLY if you're going the self-published route. Nothing makes you sound more amateur than 'THAT' used 5 times per sentence.

LDP: Laptop or desktop computer? Which do you prefer?

NC: Desktop. I hate laptops, even with a regular mouse attachment.

LDP: Do you listen to music while you write? If so, what?

NC: I listen to music all the time when I'm working on my first drafts. I especially like to listen to instrumental horror film soundtracks, but often have some of my favorite bands playing in the background. When I work on revisions, however, I have to have silence.

LDP: What time of day do you write?

NC: 90% of the time I write when I get home from work, which would be from about 5-7 PM. I'll spend another hour before bed editing or revising (usually around 11 PM-midnight). I like to write before my family has dinner as I find myself getting lazy after a nice bowl of linguini (not to mention I work a full time day job)…plus I spend a lot of time in the evening promoting my press' books and networking online.

LDP: Are you an 'in the zone' writer, or one that can sit down and write whenever you want?

NC: I CAN write almost anywhere, but prefer to be at my kitchen table on my NEO word processor before anyone gets home. I did write most of DON OF THE DEAD in my car at a local cemetery on the weekends. If you need quiet to get your final draft done, you pretty much can't beat a graveyard for silence. And the atmosphere is great.

LDP: Is there anything I didn't ask about that you would like to share with us? Any plugs?

NC: I run two blogs (one for my own writing and reviews at nickcato.blogspot.com, and one for my small press at novellopublishers.blogspot.com). I'd also like to mention an e-zine I publish titled THE HORROR FICTION REVIEW (http://www.freewebs.com/hfrzine/), which has been going strong since 2003 (the first few years as a print fanzine). Publishing this webzine is my way of relaxing, although others think it's just added work. Technically it is, but I NEED to do it.

LDP: Thank you for sharing! Best of luck with your books!

NC: My pleasure—much thanks for your time.

LDP: What type of mediums do you work with?

JC: I generally work with traditional mediums. My favorites being oil paint and ink, but I also use acrylic paint, charcoal and pencil from time to time.

LDP: What inspired you to be an artist?

JC: I've just always loved to draw. When I was really young, I would always carry a sketch book around with me and draw 24/7. When I got older, I really started to like comic book art and the art they would put on old horror and sci-fi movie posters. That's where a lot of my influence lies in my current works.

LDP: Do you feel people are born with artistic talent, or that it's something to be learned?

JC: I completely believe it's something that can be learned, but I also feel that some people are born more inclined to want to create and learn. That's where all the authors, artists, musicians, etc. come into play. We were just born wanting to create things. Other people couldn't care less and just want to watch TV.

LDP: What do you think is the biggest change from Old-world art to modern day art?

JC: With so many advances in technology, digital art is the biggest change. I just keep seeing more and more digital artists and people seem to be abandoning more traditional methods. But who can blame them? Materials are cheaper, it's less time consuming and mistakes are way easier to fix.

LDP: Do you ever use symbolism in your art?

JC: Nope, I prefer to just be straight forward in my work. There are too many pretentious artists out there. I paint what I like and that's that.

LDP: Can you think of a popular piece of art that really should be categorized as horror art?

JC: The one that immediately comes to my mind is Francisco Goya's "Saturn Devouring His Son." Plus there's a lot of religious Classical art that can come off quite eerie.

LDP: Does horror writing help you draw?

JC: A little bit. I'm always reading something and it usually falls in the horror genre, so I'll find myself doodling scenes from whatever I'm reading.

LDP: How do you feel about professional critique?

JC: Critique is good as long as it helps you improve your art in a technical aspect. But when it comes down to it, people are either going to like your art or not. So if you decide to do horror art, don't expect to be praised by the general census.

LDP: As an artist, what lured you to dabble in the macabre?

JC: When I was little I would always draw monsters, skulls, pretty much anything mean looking. I also loved watching horror movies that my older brother or sister would come home with. Eventually when I got older and got a job, I spent almost all my money on horror movies and comics.

LDP: Do you think science fiction has an influence in the horror art genera?

JC: Absolutely! Lovecraft kind of bridged those two worlds together.

LDP: What is one of your favorite horror films, and has it affected your art?

JC: I love all the classic monster movies and creature features, everything from Universal to Hammer, to '50s Sci-fi invasion movies. I'm constantly putting classic monsters in my work and for my latest project I'm going to be doing a series of Pin-up girls from all around the horror genre.

LDP: Do you aim for a specific audience, or do you feel your art may appeal to the general public?

JC: Well, I know my art doesn't appeal to the general public. That just comes with the territory. I'm mostly doing the art for myself and if like-minded people come along and enjoy it then that's all the better!

LDP: Do you think that digital art is as valid an art form as traditional mediums?

JC: If you had asked me five years ago I would have said no, but now I've grown used to it and am amazed by what people can make of a computer. Personally I'd probably get too frustrated trying to do it. So I'll stick with what I'm doing. Plus, I find there's more romance involved in traditional methods.

LDP: Like Vampires and Werewolves before them, the Zombie genre is changing in current form, what type of Zombies do you feel are scarier, running ghouls or walking ones?

JC: The only running zombies that I like were in the Return of the Living Dead series. Other than that I prefer walking ones because I find them creepier, especially Fulci's zombies.

LDP: Do you feel there is a credible difference in sensual art and pornographic art?

JC: I think there is some credible difference. Sensual art should be made in order to make some kind of statement or have elements that are aesthetically pleasing, where as pornography doesn't try all that hard. It is what it is.

LDP: Do you think that comics/graphic novels can ever be taken as a serious art form in the mainstream world of art?

JC: I can't really see it happening in the mainstream world. As I said earlier I personally love comic art and give kudos to the artists. You have to have some extreme talent to complete something like that. I would love to try to make a comic in the future but I don't feel I'm ready just yet.

LDP: Have you ever thought of making a career out of something other than art – if so, then what?

JC: I used to have pipe dreams of being a professional musician when I was in high school. I used to play in a bunch of punk rock bands. I think I was the first one to realize it's not going to happen. Plus, I thought it was too much to have to rely on the other members. With my art, I only have to rely on me.

LDP: Lastly, where can people view your art, and how can viewers buy some of your work, or contact you?

JC: My Facebook page is the most up to date and is located at:

http://www.facebook.com/horrorart
I also have a DeviantArt page here:
http://justintcoons.deviantart.com

I'm still in the process of getting some prints that will be available in the future. Follow my Facebook page if you're interested. You can find my work in the following:

• "The Junkyard" by Anthony Giangregorio (40+ illustrations by me!)

• "Undead Drive-Thru" by Rebecca Besser (cover, forthcoming)

• "Monster Party" edited by Anthony Giangregorio (cover)

• "The Undead that Saved Christmas" edited by Lyle Perez-Tinics

• "Tentacle Death Trip" by Jordan Krall (interior illustrations, forthcoming)

• Morpheus Tales issue 15, Dark Sorcery Special and Urban Horror Special

LDP: Thank for talking with us and good luck with your future projects.

JC: Thank you, it was a pleasure.

Wheels in The Sky
by Tony Schaab

I lay motionless for a moment, my eyes still closed. I can feel the pain of the crash, but it's more like a dull ache than the screaming pain I imagined it would be. I didn't think you could be driving fifty miles per hour on a winding road through the Ozarks, lose control of your car, veer off the road, have a head-on collision with a huge oak tree, all while not wearing your seat belt, and 'not' be in a fair amount of pain. I finally decide to open my eyes. Light, fluffy snowflakes swirl everywhere, making my vision seem blurry as I stare up into a bleak, cloudy sky. I'm on my back, that much is clear, but what's confusing is the fact that it's actually snowing; when I got into the accident, I was on my way home from my birthday party, and those of us born on the 4th of July don't usually get to experience winter-like conditions on the day after. Cautiously, I sit up. I don't feel or hear anything internal crunching, snapping, or making any other terrible noises, so I gingerly swivel my neck from side to side. I'm on the outskirts of a forest beside a road, possibly the one I was driving on—I'm not intimately familiar with this area—but my car is nowhere to be found. I look down at myself and am more than a little shocked to realize that I'm fine—not just a little worse for wear or slightly dinged up, but 'absolutely fine.' There's not a scratch on me, no blood anywhere. Very confusing, considering the last thing I remember is my face meeting—and blasting through—the windshield of the car. As I stand up and brush the still-falling snow off me, it's clear that I'm fine, at least physically so. What is of more pressing concern to me, however, is that as I turn to look up the road, I can see my home. There it is, seemingly less than a mile away, on a rise overlooking the valley I'm standing in, the distinctive Victorian house I grew up in. I inherited the house from my father when he passed away seven years ago, but the odd part of this isn't that I don't recognize it; it's the strangeness. Simply put, that the house shouldn't be there. It's in upstate New York, where I grew up, and the car accident I was just in happened in Missouri, where I was visiting friends. I stand on the shoulder of the road, snow swirling around me, as I look at the house in the distance. It's clearly 'my' house, I can feel it. I haven't been home in over a year, and the urge to go home wells up inside me now, more so than ever. Somehow, I know that Sherrie is still there, waiting for me. My high school sweetheart, Sherrie is truly the love of my life. I may have had commitment issues in the past, but there's nothing like the near-death experience of a car crash to put things into perspective for you. Granted, I still don't understand where my car is or why I'm not physically hurt, but those questions now take a back-seat in my mind to my primary focus: going home. The desire to walk through the front door and tell Sherrie how much she means to me is all-encompassing. The need to get to my home began as a slow burn within me, but it's now taking me over; it is truly the 'only' thing I want right now.

As if I was a robot powering up for the first time, I slowly turn my body to face the road that leads to my house on the hill, and I begin to walk. My pace quickens as the gnawing desire to reach the house continues to eat at me from within, and soon I notice I'm moving more briskly than a mall-walker out for an early-morning trot around the stores. I have also noticed that the snow, once spinning lazily in the air, also seems to have picked up its intensity, smacking my face and arms with cold, wet slaps that have started to sting a little. The house is getting closer, but it's still a ways off. The need to get there is like a hunger, eating away at my insides. I break into a jog, then into a full-on sprint, urging my legs to move in time with my resolve. The snowstorm becomes even worse, almost as if it's trying to keep me from the house. Churning sheets of white madness blanket me with their concentrated power, like a thousand tiny hands are attempting to hold me back. After running for what feels like hours, I finally come to the top of a hill, and I stop to catch my breath. Bent over with my hands on my knees, I'm intermittently panting and gulping down air like an out-of-shape grade-schooler after a particularly intense game of dodgeball. As I stand up straight again, I can see that the house is now only a few hundred feet in front of me. Relief washes over me as I think about walking through the door and telling Sherrie what I've waited far too long to tell her: that she means the world to me, that I love her, and that I never want to be without her again for as long as I live. I run to the house, too happy to mind the pelting snow anymore. I stop briefly at the end of the long, winding driveway, running my hand over the weathered old mailbox. After spending so much of my life trying to avoid being stuck in one place, working hard to get out and see the country and meet new people, I never thought it would feel 'this' good to be home. Before I can take the first step onto the driveway, I hear a noise behind me that is best described as 'unearthly.' It's an ear-piercing, cringe-inducing sound that's not unlike a thousand nails slowly running down a chalkboard, coupled with the screeching creak of someone turning a hundred-year-old valve that has long rusted shut. The atrocious noise makes my brain hurt. I quickly clasp my hands over my ears, but they do nothing to stop the onslaught of the horrible cacophony. I spin around with the intent of looking for the source of the din. It doesn't take me long. My hands drop to my sides as I look up and stare, dumbfounded. I don't know why I haven't seen this before. There, suspended in the sky, is what I can only describe as a gigantic wheel. An archaic stone ring with vicious-looking spiked spokes, the massive wheel defies every law of physics I know by simply hanging there in the evening sky. The terrible sound is being made as the wheel turns, slowly at first, then moving faster. As the wheel turns, my vision becomes shaky. It seems as if the entire world is stretching, flattening itself; the more the wheel turns, the more the space around me seems to be losing a dimension. I also feel like I'm being flattened, pulled in two different directions, like baker's dough being stretched too thin. I turn back to face my house, only to see that it is now moving away from me! The 'stretching' of the world is pulling the property off into the distance. I try to move towards it, but the pain being caused by the bending of space is too much for me to go more than a few paces before falling to my knees in anguish.

I cry out, partly because of the pain and partly because I was so close to being home again, which is now the only thing in the world that I want. As the pain intensifies and the noise increases to a deafening volume, I collapse on the ground, closing my eyes and gritting my teeth in aguish. 'This' is what I imagine the car crash would feel like. Then, as quickly as it started, the noise stops and the pain is gone. I lay motionless for a moment, my eyes still closed. Quickly, I snap them open as I scramble to my feet. Now that the pain and noise are gone, perhaps I can still make it to my home! I look around eagerly as I stand up, and I once again I am confused and in disbelief as to what I see. The dreary day of snow is gone, erased like it never existed. The summer sun is beating down on me intensely, beads of sweat already forming on my lip and brow. I'm standing on the side of a dusty road, surrounded by desert as far as I can see. I look up to the sky and see the gigantic wheel hanging above me. Large and silent, it simply sits there, as if defying me to question its existence. At least it's not moving, and making the disastrous sound that seems to come with its turning. And once again, miles up the road, off in the distance I can see my home. Even though it's so far away, I know immediately what it is; it's the only structure I can see, and my desire to go there hasn't diminished in the least. Confused and disoriented, I do the only thing I can think to do: I begin to walk, starting the long journey to the house. After a while, I begin to run, in an attempt to get there more quickly; it's a futile endeavor. The already-sweltering heat permeates every inch of the air, and it seems that the more I try to run, the hotter it actually becomes. I plod along, exhausted but not willing to stop. The house is still a good distance away, but I see something ahead on the opposite side of the road. I'm not sure what it is, and I don't know quite what to expect; I'm surprised at how easily the rational part of my brain has decided to shut down and simply accept all of these strange occurrences. I have no idea what's happening to me, but what I do know is that I need to get to my house in order to feel happy and content again. I slowly walk up to the objects on the side of the road: a simple blue postal mailbox and a desk, one of the small, elementary school styles with the desktop attached directly to the chair. On top of the desk is a single piece of blank paper with a silver pen and a clay pencil beside it. Not knowing what else to do, I sit down at the desk. My hand hovers over both writing utensils for a moment before picking up the silver pen. As if in a trance, I begin to write. I'm composing a letter to Sherrie. The writing flows freely, and I fill up the entire front and back of the sheet with words about how much I miss her, how I hate that I've taken her love for me for granted for so long, and how I want nothing more than to come home and show her how much I love her. I tell her I will be home soon, and that I hope she can wait a little longer until I arrive. When I'm done writing, I fold the paper in half and put it in the large blue mailbox. Even though there is no envelope or address, I feel confident the letter will reach her.

Inspired and re-energized, I begin to sprint to the house. I can feel it getting closer, and even though I'm close to physical exhaustion and probable heat stroke, I carry on. Time has lost all meaning. I feel like I have been moving towards the house under the hot summer sun for days, not stopping to rest, eat, or sleep. Finally, I find myself once again only a few feet from the end of the driveway, the house now looming large in front of me. I breathe a sigh of relief as I begin to walk up the driveway. Suddenly and without warning, the terrible noise begins again. Slowly at first, the screeching seems to float down from the sky and wash over me in a wave of sound. Mentally and physically exhausted, I turn my head to the heavens to stare at the wheel. The monstrosity stares back at me without eyes. It has begun to turn, slowly moving in place, and once again I can feel my body begin to stretch and flatten out, along with the rest of the world. As I cringe from the pain that begins to envelop me, I turn to look back at my house, already knowing what I'm going to see. Sure enough, my home is moving away from me, stretching off into the horizon as if taunting me to try and catch it. The frustration of the situation washes over me. I want to pump my fists and scream at the wheel, but the pain is too great. I stumble as I double over, my arms stopping me from falling entirely. I grimace in anguish, closing my eyes tightly. I'm full of torment, both internal and external. I can't tell if my face is wet from my sweat, tears, or a mixture of both. The cacophony of sound becomes all-encompassing, and I'm smashed face-down to the ground, as if I only exist in two dimensions. Just when I feel the pain is too much to bear...it all stops. The pain and the noise are gone, like someone flipped a giant switch and made it all disappear. I lay motionless for a moment, my eyes still closed. I feel wetness on my face. Slowly, I open my eyes and roll over so I'm laying face-up on the ground. It's raining; the kind of rain that stings your skin ever-so-slightly, not enough to truly hurt but just enough to be an annoyance. I have gone from lying on the hot, dry, dusty earth a moment ago to now lying on a patch of grass and feeling a slight chill from the incessant rain. Staring up at the sky, I shift my eyes and turn my head slightly to the right, already knowing what I'm going to see. The giant stone wheel is there. It seems to be independent of the weather, as if it were above the rain clouds but still perfectly visible in its corner of the sky. I sigh dejectedly as I stare at it. What is it? Why is it tormenting me? Who controls it? And more importantly, why does it seem to be trying to keep me from my home, my true happiness? That final thought sends a surge of energy through me. I stand up and take a look at my surroundings. I'm in the middle of a grassy field that seems to stretch on to the horizon. As I spin around, I once more set my sights upon the object of my desire: there in the distance, my home sits. It almost feels as if it's calling to me on a subconscious level, urging me to come to it, even though I know, invariably, that I won't be able to reach it. I'm not sure I will ever make it home again. Still...I must try. The rain still falling, I begin my trek through the field, my feet sloshing through the wet grass.

I walk without urgency at first, for based on my last few excursions, I believe I have all the time I need to get from here to there, not that I have any concept of time anymore. It feels like only a moment since all this started, but it also feels like it's been going on forever. I'm truly lost and confused, but I must carry on; I have nothing else to keep me sane. After a while, the house seems to grow closer, and I almost let myself believe I can see Sherrie through the large bay window on the front porch. With a renewed sense of longing, I begin to run through the tall grass, and as I do the rain begins to fall harder. Soon, I'm running at full-steam through sheets of sleet that seem to intentionally try to knock me off-balance. After a while, I do lose my footing, tripping and falling. I land head-first in the grass, sliding to a stop with my arms in front of me like a baseball player reaching for home plate. I am physically and mentally exhausted. My nerves are shot, and I feel like I want to scream in anger and cry in submission all at the same time. I don't understand why this is happening to me! I raise my head and see a familiar sight: my mailbox and the end of the driveway are just a few short feet away from me. Before I can even process the thought to stand, I hear the sound I already know was coming. The screeching is as horrible as it was when I first heard it, what seems confusingly like ages and only minutes ago. Dejected and mentally preparing for the inevitable pain and stretching that is sure to come, I flop onto my back, arms and legs outstretched, and close my eyes in my emotional and physical exhaustion. The horrible sound increases in volume and intensity, and even though my eyes are closed, it seems as if the image of the gigantic wheel turning in the sky is etched in fire in my mind. The numbing pain stabs me suddenly and intensely. As my body stretches beyond what is physically possible, I can feel my prize, my destination, moving away from me once more; the feelings of utter despair and desolation encompass my entire being. Suddenly, it dawns on me through the pain: I know what's happening to me. I know what's going on, where I am, and why I'm being besieged. I died in the car crash. Now I'm in Hell. My own, personal Hell. Just like Tantalus from ancient Greek mythology, who spent an eternity in the underworld being deathly thirsty but unable to take a drink, even though he was up to his neck in water, I'm being punished by having what I want dangled in front of me. I'm doomed to constantly try and reach my home and my love, only to have them forever yanked away from me, in a manner most painful to my mind, my soul, and my body. As I come to this realization, the pain and the noise suddenly stop. I'd like to think, that I have figured out what's going on, that they are gone for good, but I immediately know in my heart that is not the case. I am in Hell, and will be here forever. There is no red demon with horns and a pitchfork, there's something much, much worse. The constant reminder that I will never again have what I want the most, what I squandered in life and am now doomed to forever repeat in death. Even though I keep my eyes closed, I can feel the morning sun on my face, and I know I have switched locations once more.

I lay motionless for a moment, my eyes still closed. And though I can't see it, I know the wheel in the sky sits above, waiting to turn again.

DARK RIDDLE
A SON OF GOTHICANE

FAQ: I'll start with some of the obvious questions then. They say you're from the ghetto, but some even say you came from "beneath" the ghetto, why is that? And where did you learn Hypergothics and how did it get used in Chicago's culture?

Dark Riddle: That question is one of the most that people ask me, yet it seems everybody knows that answer by now. I'm from Little Village and Pilsen, along with my older BTB brethren –the ones referred to as "Templar" BTBs –meaning that they're not mid-generation or new school BTBs, but the ones from the original Temple so to speak. During the '80s, people like Worm, Jinxster, Roxski, Johnny Cool, Salski, and me would take care of abandoned buildings for slumlords. Essentially, we were entrusted to keep out scrap raiders that would usually reduce these buildings to skeletons, while their owners were trying to get their buildings up to code. One such building grew quite popular before it was knocked down in the '90s. Locals called it the "Body Rock" club, because we invited all our b-boy friends and Zulu brothers to practice the Hip Hop arts there. We mediated for this large building for years and it was a second home for us, especially during Chicago's harsh winters.

FAQ: So Hypergothics came from there, abandoned buildings?

Dark Riddle: Well, partially, but no. It really came from what is known today as "Gothicane". Gothicane is a general term usually used most by north side Goths. It's a coined name that refers to several areas of Chicago that fall under the Gothicane culture. The term allegedly came from the Finch family way back at the turn-of-the-century. It's said that Mary Finch first coined that name in 1945, but more recently us Darks, Reds, and Slims popularized it. Most of these areas are underground storerooms, tunnels, and the basement portions of abandoned buildings. Together, they stretch far and wide around the city, and housed a unique set of people that live there. It's from these extraordinary people that I learned the essentials of not only the Gothicane culture and Templaric religious beliefs, but also the cryptic rights to Hypergothics and its uses.

FAQ: Did Gothicane include Al Capone's tunnels?

By Jesus Morales AKA "Dark Riddle"

Dark Riddle: Nope. That's one of the biggest myths about Gothicane. AL Capone's tunnels were "not" and never have been a part of Gothicane, even in the old age.

FAQ: Does Gothicane exist today?

Dark Riddle: Only parts of it do. Gothicane was basically composed of four regional areas; Sub-Cermak, West End, Canel Street Enclave, and Golgotha. Some parts of Sub-Cermak are still accessible and so are parts of Canal Street's tunnel ways, but places like Golgotha and West End are completely abandoned and many of the portholes were cemented up during the mid '90s.

FAQ: Why was Gothicane abandoned and who closed off the areas?

Dark Riddle: You know, there's still controversy over why it was targeted and closed down, but since I was a "Dark" even then, and fought to keep Gothicane alive during the mid '80s to early '90s, I have my own ideas about that. Gothicane was basically made up of four sects that believed in the same religious ideology and cultural genera. Although each group was dedicated to certain creeds, we basically got along very well. In fact, once you were accepted in the underground, you were obligated to abide by their rules, which to ground level people, certainly seemed taboo to say the least. Gothicane was around for at least 80 years.

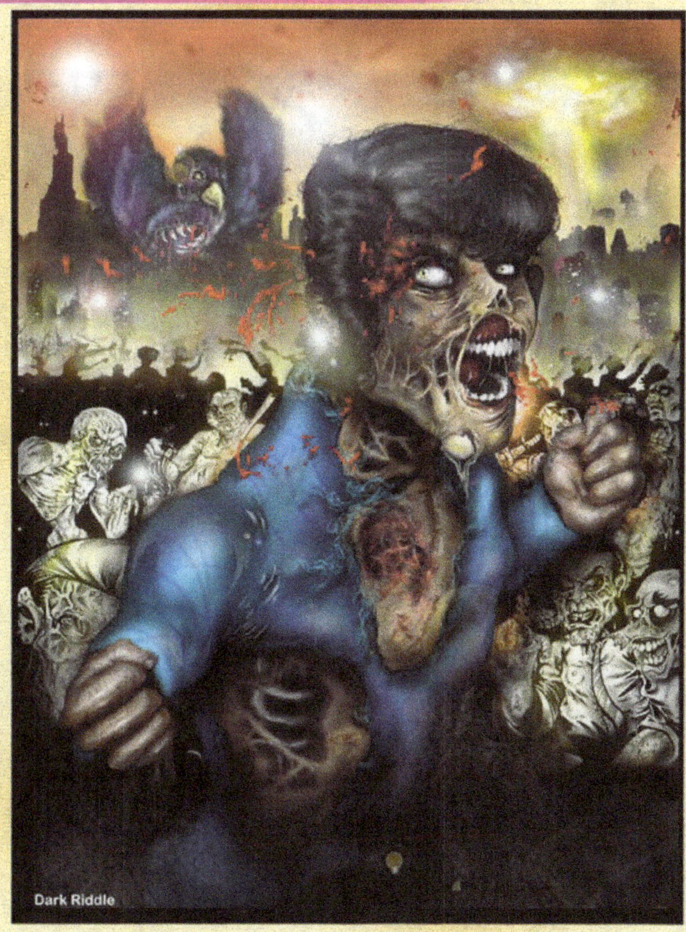

It expanded during the '50's when places such as Lawrence Fisheries moved and left behind, yet again, more underground storerooms and access ways. But in hindsight, I feel that Gothicane's fall came from winter. You see, for decades, Gothicane's underground society was actually powered by what I think were city generators. It's said, that the first residents of Gothicane were moved from a now abandoned mental institution called the Chicago State Hospital, or more infamously known as Dunning. This was done in some kind of city-spawned project to get the patients outside of the overcrowded asylum and back into society, while doing work for the city.

FAQ: So Gothicane's foundation was built on the mentally ill. It was made by crazy people!?!

Dark Riddle: Well, yes. For lack of a better term, that would be a true statement. But these people were an innovative group, many consisting of bipolar savants with a wide range of exceptional talents. As time passed, they began expanding Gothicane through deals with slumlords and the discovery of old tunnels and archways in Chicago's underground, securing and renovating each section as they collected territory. So, by the 1960's Gothicane had grown into a large enough society to house four groups, the Reds, the Slims, the Sabbat, and the Darks. But when social workers failed to keep charities going and discontinued funding for Gothicane, the 17 generators used to power Gothicane were turned off. This didn't kill Gothicane, but made it weak. Eventually it got weak enough to become susceptible to attack from one of its own sects…the Sabbat.

FAQ: Why was the power shut off?

Dark Riddle: Again, that's a debatable issue. Eventually it was turned back on after a horrific uprising between the cults had occurred, due to the Sabbat, wanting to take over the underground and its collection of slumlord clients. But by then, the damage and people injured was far too extensive to be revamped. This was an odd circumstance, because for years and years, social workers would check up on Gothicane's residents to make sure their needs were met.

But even they had predicted to the higher-ups that turning off the generators might make Gothicane fall to an aggressive sect. This did happen, until the Sabbat were cornered into extinction by the Templar Darks.

Dark Riddle: Obviously, before me was Dark Ripper, but in chronological order it goes as follows: Dark Raine, Dark Terra, Dark Fayde, Dark Vexson, Dark Ripper, and Dark Rex. I come after Rex, actually I was his "replacement". After me comes Dark Sable and Dark Synge, then the so-called BTB Darks such as Dark Stare and Dark Jerne.

Dark Riddle: I was doing graffiti and was already quite known as a skillful street artist at the time. This was around 1988 and I had done some notable pieces with Salksi and Roxski on places like McCormick school and the Hall of Fame. So the graffiti power was already established when I was sent to join the other Darks against the perverted actions of the Sabbat. This series of fights would later become known as "The Nausicaan Uprising." That name was probably derived from Sabbat agents like Henry Nausicaa and his cronies such as Black Light Bobby, and Black Corben.

But eventually they were defeated through a pretty smart strategy by one of my mentors called Dark Ripper. Since the Sabbat had adopted an opposite ideology from, Reds, Slims, and Darks, they became very dangerous and we all knew they had to be extinguished fairly fast. But it was only when Dark Ripper cut them off from all of their financing, and recruited enough Darks to not only physically overpower them, but destroy their ideology, too, did their extinction finally occur. Graffiti art played a weird role in the underground; because it was used to apply important symbols on parts of Gothicane that indicated where and when a certain sect had been taken over. It also acted as a simple code to where and when Reds or Darks would be coming back.

Dark Riddle: Surprisingly, no. But the fights were brutal and torturous. The Sabbat had changed while the others sects were not paying attention. While we were being complacent, they had changed their creed and motto to "Do as you will", which was a dead give-a-way that they were turning Luciferian. They were basically mixing a lot of their ideology with perverse cults such as Crowley's and Anton Levay's. Normally this kind of thing would be of little concern as many Luciferians practice simple rebellion ideals, but for the Sabbat, which already had roots from a history of violent mental compulsions – this new found ideology could be down right deadly.

Alien Spider Woman: A Posessed "Un-Thing" from "Empire of Dirt"   Art by Dark Riddle

Dark Riddle: Well, the people there, were and are, still bizarre compared to ground level people. But you have to remember, they were brought there and later on as they reproduced, most of the time with their own kind, they evolved rituals and traditions that don't apply to the surface world. As for Gothicane, it's not as it is now, mostly abandoned and filled with dirt and grime. In fact, there's a shocking similarity between how Gothicane looks and the video game "Bio-Shock", which might not be a coincidence. Gothicane's hey-day and its current renovations are all based on the 1920's style archways and retro-future architecture they built way back then. In the video game Bio-Shock, designers made a surprisingly similar look for the game; and if you watch the names on the game's credits, you'll see that some of them match exactly with artists that once roamed Gothicane in real life. Yet even so, they are Chicagoans - true Chicagoans and a little known part of our city's history. As for Gothicane's groups, the Reds are an all-female sect that had populated the part of Gothicane called West End. They're easy to distinguish because they look very Gothic, but instead of being fragile or Emo, they are obsessed with athleticism. Many of them, despite their apparent beauty, are unpredictable and often throw violent fits –though as to why, I have no idea. But like Darks their tradition mandates that they carry the word "Red" in their name. This is why every Red uses that suffix at the end of their name.

Dark Riddle: Exactly. In the same way, Darks use the prefix word "Dark" in front of their name. This is why my full street name is Dark Riddle. This tradition gets passed on to other Darks as they learn the secrets of the Dark Arts. Reds have a weird motto they uphold: Manipulation, Illusion, and Humanities. Darks have a more understandable one: Art, Literature, and science. But Slims are probably the most bizarre of the entire community. Slims are extremely emasculate men - or women that are somewhat boy-like. Out of the 18 I know of, they are all androgynous, meaning that it is hard to decipher their genders.

Though many of them are gay, many are not. In particular, and probably the most known of the Slims, are Dark Sable and Cora the Red. Despite being men-like, they look like small, skinny females with very wide eyes and feline-like faces. The weird thing about them is they're like this naturally, without any make-up or surgery. Just as some victims of Downs Syndrome have a certain set of physical traits, Slims with CAIS disease have oddly attractive wide eyes and triangular, almost-feline-like faces. I had thought for a long time, that they inducted the most feminine looking men to encompass their group. They might have done that on occasion. But by far, I believe that they are the by-products of incestuous offspring. Basically, that they are indeed "partially" in-bred females or possibly true hermaphrodites, or in Dark Sable's case, genuinely female yet "Intersexed." Because this is so rare and misunderstood, agencies interested in this particular group put up most of the money to keep what remains of Gothicane alive. So it's the odd nature of the Slims that support what's left of Gothicane.

Dark Riddle: I really can't say. I know there are Intersex groups in San Fransisco, Florida, and New York. You have to remember, 1 out of every 2 thousand births is an intersex child to some degree, so the condition is not rare. What is very rare is the grouping or occult grouping of them. Each group has a particular look and tradition. However, those outside of Chicago don't call themselves Slims. It's a controversial issue because some doctors call the condition, especially CAIS, the type most Gothicane Slims are affected with, a real disease. But I don't know if that's true. That's like telling a dwarf or "Little Person" that they suffer from a disease, which could be slander to their kind. It would appear to me, that Intersex people vary from group to group and uphold their own culture according to their locale. For example, in Chicago Slims almost always have a short "Bob" hair cut. This is done to purposely make deciphering their gender even harder. This freakish defense mechanism works quite well, because people tend to leave them alone since they don't know how to act towards such androgynous folks.

Dark Riddle: Yes…don't go there, watch the Chicago episodes of the cable show called "Urban Explorers" and you'll get to see many parts of it, without being arrested. Gothicane is largely City-Owned and the parts that might still be accessible are probably impassible now, so it would be illegal to visit them today. More so, West End is a particularly scary place even for us, because it's used as a sanctuary for suicidal Reds and Darks that can't control their often-violent compulsions. Since West End is the only traditionally cultural area for suicides, it's a very frightening place that still haunts the underworld through modern myths. It's not a good place to be. But on the bright side, Gothicane has direct and interesting ties to iconic places such as Dunning Mental Asylum, the Graffiti Hall of Fame, and several Skid-Rows. So, on a social and psychological level, it's extremely attractive for people interested in a real life culture that has a very haunting presence in Chicago history.

Note: Gothicane Art & Culture are practiced by a wide variety of writers & artists often considered "Occult" however no persons mentioned here are labeled, nor necessarily considered "Cultists".

GOTHIC ZOMBIE GIRL BY DARK RIDDLE JESUS MORALES…BTB CREW

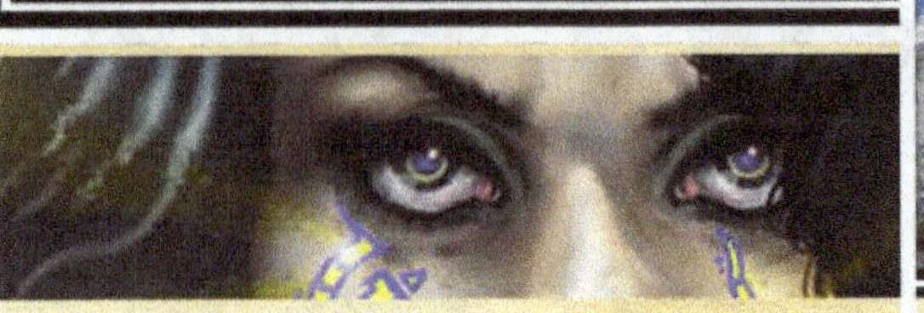

www.ingramcontent.com/pod-product-compliance
Lightning Source LLC
Chambersburg PA
CBHW082103090726
47910CB00008B/2581